MW01707957

Between 2 Worlds, 2 Men

# Via Roma

ESSENTIAL PROSE SERIES 117

Canada Council for the Arts
Conseil des Arts du Canada

ONTARIO ARTS COUNCIL
CONSEIL DES ARTS DE L'ONTARIO
an Ontario government agency
un organisme du gouvernement de l'Ontario

Canada

Guernica Editions Inc. acknowledges the support of the Canada Council for the Arts and the Ontario Arts Council. The Ontario Arts Council is an agency of the Government of Ontario.

We acknowledge the financial support of the Government of Canada.
Nous reconnaissons l'appui financier du gouvernement du Canada.

# Between 2 Worlds, 2 Men

# Via Roma

## Mary Melfi

GUERNICA EDITIONS
TORONTO • BUFFALO
• LANCASTER (U.K.)
2015

Michael Mirolla, editor
David Moratto, cover & interior design
Guernica Editions Inc.
1569 Heritage Way, Oakville, (ON), Canada L6M 2Z7
2250 Military Road, Tonawanda, N.Y. 14150-6000 U.S.A.
www.GuernicaEditions.com

Distributors:
University of Toronto Press Distribution,
5201 Dufferin Street, Toronto (ON), Canada M3H 5T8
Gazelle Book Services, White Cross Mills, High Town,
Lancaster LA1 4XS U.K.

First edition.
Printed in Canada.

Legal Deposit—Third Quarter
Library of Congress Catalog Card Number: 2015936499
Library and Archives Canada Cataloguing in Publication
Melfi, Mary, 1951-, author
Via Roma : between 2 worlds, 2 men / Mary Melfi. -- 1st edition.

(Essential prose series ; 117)
Issued in print and electronic formats.
ISBN 978-1-77183-014-0 (pbk.).--ISBN 978-1-77183-015-7 (epub).--
ISBN 978-1-77183-016-4 (mobi)

I. Title. II. Series: Essential prose series ; 117

PS8576.E46V53 2015 C813'.54 C2015-902303-3 C2015-902304-1

The author gratefully acknowledges
the financial assistance from
*Le Conseil des arts et des letters du Québec.*

PART I

# Wedding Albums

*How many angels are there?*
*One, who transforms our lives, is plenty.*
—A TRADITIONAL SAYING

# Chapter 1

How is this possible? Suddenly the world looks more as it should: full of promise and merriment and baby blue skies; the prodigal sun has found its way back home eager to settle down and work wonders, changing the colour of my sad thoughts, and all because my eyes have met his for the first time.

"I know you," he tells me and I agree, even though I actually never saw him before, was never in Florence in the *Piazza del Duomo*, supposedly in tears because the B*attistero di San Giovanni* was then closed for repairs.

Stepping onto the dance floor of a small restaurant in Little Italy and almost immediately tripping, my dance instructor tells me to relax.

"Anyone can tango," he assures me. "It's not a dance for the high and mighty."

I laugh. He doesn't.

The tango was born in the slums of *Buenos Aires*, he reminds me. A lot of Italians lived there at the turn of the last century; why even his great grandfather called it home for awhile. During the day the Italian émigrés dug ditches, paved roads, and landscaped the homes of the rich. At night they crowded together in the streets, playing cards, drinking wine, sharing food and news from home. Sometimes the men danced, often with each other. (Few women made the long trek to South America at the time.) Waltzes and polkas were all the rage then, but these dances didn't capture the mood of the *birds of passage*. So their accordionists improvised, creating their own musical language—the language of flight. Of migration. If you listen carefully to the tango, you can hear the loneliness and confusion of a new arrival.

I agree. The tango expresses nostalgia. And sadness.

"When you tango," my instructor tells me, leading me, or trying to lead me across the room, "you move from one area to the next. You're retracing your steps. Going from one country to another. Suddenly, everything is different—the food, the language, the smells. You're not sure if you like the new place or not. What do you do? You regress. Like a child you stamp your feet and complain. Go ahead—stamp your feet!"

I do as I am told with predictable results—my dance instructor's feet get amply stamped on. (I shouldn't have worn heels!)

Undeterred, he continues the lesson. I turn every which way but the right way, bumping into tables and chairs and waiters and bus boys, proving I'm *The Champion of Left Feet*.

"Don't worry," he insists. "Anyone can learn the steps."

Anyone and everyone, but me! If I were an immigrant,

I might learn how to tango, but I am a native-born Canadian. (What do I know?)

At heart everyone's an immigrant, I'm told. Everyone is on a quest for self-improvement. Even if you live in one city all your life, you can still get lost in it. You still need directions, hope. Social mobility.

So think of the tango as a war dance, I'm told. It prepares you for battle. It fills you with self-delusions. Nothing can hurt you. You can move from one battlefield to another, exchange one world for another, unscathed. When you dance, you're as much a god as you'll ever be.

I agree. You can't be a workhorse all your life and not rebel. Make dance, not war, I agree.

In dance is our redemption, I agree. Still, I can't tell my right foot from my left.

"It's my fault," he says. "I'm not a dance instructor. I'm filling in for my dad. He owns this place."

His eyes convince me I'm beautiful. Thank heavens lust is blind and there is a sudden downpour of rain, and heaven knows I shouldn't invite him to my place but I do. Sex can't cure the common cold, but it can beat the blues, and as for love, well, it's as potent as poison, which is to say: "Watch out, Sophie Wolfe!"

You can go around the world in 80 days and return to the exact same spot you started, lonelier than ever; luckily, it didn't happen to me. My lover contains the Seven Wonders of the World.

Each time I visit him, I am amazed he lets me in. He laughs and I laugh and the room laughs. The windows are open even when they're closed. When he is in the room, I breathe easily. The sun shows off. The stars show off. The music begins or the sex; it doesn't matter which comes first. He radiates acceptance; he spoon-feeds me happiness.

I love everything about him. The way he thinks. The way he looks. The way he wraps his arms around me and makes me feel safe. I love the sound of his name; even when a stranger says it: "*Dante Aglieri,*" I get goose bumps. There are dozens of businesses in Little Italy named after Italy's greatest poet, Dante Alighieri: *Pizzeria Dante*, *Pasticceria Dante* and *Café Via Dante,* but not any of them exude *The Divine Comedy* (Part 3: Celestial Bliss) as does this man whom I now claim as my own.

I want to know everything about him—take in his personal history (inhale his thoughts if I could). I know what the situation is. (You can't be with someone 80 days and not know it)—he is an architect, a good one, but he had to quit his job to help out his parents. He'll do anything to make sure the bank (or is it the Mafia he's worried about?) doesn't shut down his parents' restaurant, *Chez Nina*.

"We can't afford a house—not yet," the 29-year-old lets me know, as if I needed to be bribed. As if I would need more than the joy of him.

"Teach me Italian," I say, eager to embrace his 2,000-year-old culture. Mine's too young.

"I'll teach you Italian but don't expect me to teach you to love me," he replies. "You'll have to do that on your own."

The scent of his flesh—his intelligence!—drives me wild. I hunger for his touch, his spirit, his acknowledgment. Others have taken a liking to my body, one (a Dr. Guido Cotroni) even satisfied my primitive craving to be loved, but not like this man! Knowing him has eliminated the competition. Cupid is as efficient as a hit man.

Mr. Dante Aglieri has introduced new blood into my veins; added some sort of iron—spirit iron. No other man has revolutionized the way I think so thoroughly. Sophie Wolfe was a 28-year-old salesclerk in an antique shop and now she's Wonder Woman!

"Love me and my love will envelop the city like a bullet-proof vest," I joke. "Love me and my love will soften up the crime bosses. It's too nice a day to hurt anyone. Love me and I will enjoy a good meal, a good cup of coffee, do the ordinary things as if it were my last day on earth. And that's no joke."

"You're so pretty," he says. "Everyone should have a girl like you. My angel of love."

I let him sweet talk me; I can't get enough of it.

His love fills me up with holiness. That's right—holiness. His love is holy like the sun, the moon, artificial light are holy. His love is holy like my unholy desire to live forever. It can't be done, but when I'm with him, I want it.

In the 80 days we've known each other, he has transformed the little island I live on, *la Ville de Montréal*, into The City of God.

"Marry me," he says, washing my feet with his tongue, washing the air with his words.

As if his words were a chant, a prayer, a litany of good tidings, I respond to them without thought or hesitation: "Oh yes, my sweet friend, I give myself to thee!"

I wish him happiness; I wish myself happiness. The world was his and now it is mine.

While the Aglieris are busy entertaining each other, busily enjoying the four (or is it six?) course restaurant meal, busily enjoying the piped-in band's rendition of "A Stranger in Paradise," my fiancé (there I said it—fiancé!) slowly and without urgency, as if we had the rest of our lives (we do have the rest of lives!) pulls down my lace panties. (Of course, they're lace. I bought them precisely for him to remove them!) I knew this would happen, I just hadn't expected it to happen in his parents' restaurant, in the kitchen, next to the wood-fired oven, around closing time.

Standing against the wall, it's quite comfortable, it's romantic even, though it's as far removed from a matrimonial bed as an astronaut walking in space—I could be walking in space, there's not enough air (It's easy to choke up on love); a space suit would come in handy and he offers me one—falls on his knees and places his tongue in just the right place, and that helps me breathe better (and how!). Soon, I'm the one who unzips his pants and aggressively takes charge. This is the moment I've been waiting for all my life, this is it. I am no longer some daddy's little girl. I'm a woman now, cocksure of her rights. I insist he give me pleasure, insist his hands discover my body and remould it to suit *my* needs. I'm strong enough for it. My body is in readiness for more kisses and caresses, no matter the dishwasher makes noise and the smell of the soup of the day is too close for comfort, all I hear and smell is my own desire. Am poisoned with the wish to be eternally his, poisoned with the wish for eternal love, eternal communion, eternal fucking. That's it! When you're in love, eternity is at your fingertips. It doesn't matter if it is or it isn't, you wish it, and that's enough.

My panties off, my skirt pulled up, I fit him in, and two become one. Enjoy maximum understanding, maximum cooperation, maximum pleasure, though pleasure is too small a word to contain what I experience, as he controls me and I control him; are two at the helm of a star ship. His tenderness is my lifeboat—I am anchored by it. (Come now, how can tenderness be a lifeboat and an anchor? Thought you were walking in space?) Well, mixed metaphors happen when you're hot for each other. Can't think straight when any time now a busboy or a waiter, or heaven forbid, his dad or mom will walk in on us and be convinced all-Canadian girls are *bad*, if *bad* means horny and horny means can't be satisfied, but then, I can be (satisfied). Besides, I'm dressed and he's dressed, and we're safely hidden behind a stack of dirty dishes.

Everything changes when you're this hungry. Common sense starts to make no sense; un-common sense rules here, and it's ever so beautiful, ever so sweet. Love is the ultimate artificial sweetener; it can sweeten the act of coming together like nothing else. Hate fattens you up with rage but love deflates the ego, and so you end up lighter—egoless and satisfied. Actually love can make your flesh taste sweeter than it is. Love is a no-nonsense joyful fruit salad, a real dish; all verbs and nouns and thoughts have a fruity taste when you are in love. Actually what takes place is the sacrament the holy books call for when a man and woman are joined together. The act is accomplished like a symphony is accomplished with the cooperation of a master conductor and composer, or like a watercolour is accomplished. Like any good thing, the act is accomplished easily; no effort is involved (this is a labour of love!); no supervisors are involved and no performance reviews will be handed out. There will be no checking up on how ridiculous you look sweaty and smelly. (Who cares?) Unlike a business merger which is accomplished with a lot of fanfare, our union is celebrated without anyone noticing. (What a blessing!)

My fiancé kisses my panties before he gives them back to me and I thank him.

# Chapter 2

On the table: accusations. Questions of impropriety. Infidelity!

What can I say? An *old* love is like a basket of rose petals—each petal is a miniature testament of goodwill; a *new* love is like a rose with magical properties—pull its petals apart and the flower can be put back together.

"You should have warned me," says my old flame, the dentist, Dr. Guido Cotroni, and he's right, but after dating him for four and a half years, I couldn't bring myself to tell him to his face: "It's over!" So, I left the message on his answering machine. I could have emailed him and said something like: "You're married; he isn't." But what good would it have done? I deceived him.

"I never ever, imagined you to be so bad," he says. "I gave you my heart, and it has been my misfortune. You have been with this man for over two months, and you never, ever said a word. I had no clue. You seemed so sincere. Serene. Loyal! How did you manage it? You fucked him one night, and me, the next? Is there an app on your iPad on how to get away with murder?"

I wish I could turn myself into a flower so I wouldn't have to talk. But even silence can be used as a blunt instrument. It can hurt like hell.

"I've been faithful to you," he says.

Sure he has. The man parcelled out his affection like a pay cheque. He wouldn't see me more than twice a month.

"That was your fault," he insists. "You never asked for anything."

I was as reliable as a whore, I admit.

"Why are you doing this, Sophie?"

As many reasons as there are raindrops, but I keep them to myself.

Even if he were to get on his knees and plead: "Don't go. I want nothing, nothing else than you not to leave me, because without you I won't know how to live. I will die if you leave me." I would still walk out the door.

You can't love and lack courage.

Someone taps me on the shoulder and says: "When someone you love dies plant a fruit-bearing tree at his gravesite. If the dead can smell flowers, don't you think they can eat?"

And then I wake up.

On the corner of *rue Saint-Paul* and *rue Saint-François-Xavier* in *le Vieux-Montréal* stands the antique shop I work in.

Each time I open it, I enter a magic world filled with old clocks, onyx pedestals, crystal, silverware, $17^{th}$ and $18^{th}$ century chairs and commodes. I'm Alice in Wonderland and this is my rabbit hole.

When the weather is good and sales are up, and the owner of the shop is attending an auction or an estate sale, as he is today, there's no other place in the world I would rather be. Every object in this shop has an added layer of sacredness, because it once belonged to someone who passed away. Their spirit lingers. Get in touch with it, and you commune with the dead, who can be as nice as any of us.

The dead are willing to share their stories. If you listen carefully, your IQ increases a wee bit. It has to. It doesn't matter if the original owner of the $17^{th}$ century hand-carved boudoir love seat I'm resting on was brilliant or inept, the fact is he has crossed over to the Otherworld. And so his knowledge of life has been enhanced. Otherworldly travels can turn an ordinary man into an exceptional one. (This I believe.) Jesus Christ spoke in parables, but so do the dead; listen and be enlightened ...

No time for reflection. Clients a-ringing. Client No. 1: "Be looking for Elvis busts."

No Elvises on the premises. (Sorry.) Life-size plastic busts of the king of rock and roll or statuettes of Madonna, the pop idol, or of the Virgin Mary can't be found here. Nor are nostalgia collectibles available. I send the Elvis-devotee to Montréal's Antique Alley over on *rue Notre-Dame.* There the shelves are overflowing with cheap nostalgia goods: Zippo lighters, depression era glassware, hip flasks, cookie jars (The Queen Mother of Talk Shows, Oprah Winfrey, is a known collector), Victorian dolls and wind-up toys. If you're not a serious collector on the hunt for big ticket items, don't enter this shop. There should be a sign on the door: FOR RICH PEOPLE ONLY.

Client No. 2 claims he once bought a 20,000-year-old Palaeolithic carving for 50 dollars. He's disappointed he can't find another in my shop.

Client No. 3, a telepath, reads my thoughts: everyone and everything deserves a second chance. That's why, she says, she likes antique shops so much. Here old things are given a new life. An antique clock or a watch doesn't even have to tell the time to be valued. It's good as is. The telepath's Alabama accent intimidates me, but not so much that I can't ring up the cash register.

And the day continues; the sun appears, disappears. A real vanishing act. The clock strikes six and the next man to walk through the door is no client at all, but my kindred spirit, my beautiful husband-to-be.

This is heaven: waking up satisfied, having had more than a good night's rest, your body's delicious capacity for entertainment noted and made use of. One minute you're on the bed, your tongue hanging out like a joyless dog, and the next, magic sounds come out of your mouth—you could be an opera singer, given the opportunity. Okay, you don't have much of a voice, but who cares? A tongue works wonders. You don't have to die to go to heaven; an orgasm will do just as nicely.

This is heaven: when the joy of sex doesn't capture the half of it; when you're in love, you're filled up with the joy of the mundane. You can wash dishes and not be bothered, can shake off the rain from an umbrella and think it fun; you can even consider there might be joy in being a servant even though you never gave it much thought and if you had, you wouldn't have thought it likely anyone could take much pleasure in giving up his body for someone else. (Now you know better.)

This is heaven: his body, his kiss, your bed.

This is heaven: waking up, indifferent to noise. Not being alone, you gladly avoid confrontations with aggressive machines. Cars and oil tankers and Greyhound buses and wailing ambulances and speeding taxis are racing down the street; airplanes, traffic helicopters and unknown flying objects are racing across the skyway. But do you care? You don't hear a thing; even the kitchen sink's no-nonsense drip is silenced, because of the noise your body makes when he notices you, noticing him. Extracting the same pleasure as a painter putting a dash of blue on his muddy replica of the sky (Earth's happy roof), you find God, or rather, the joy of everything.

This is heaven: him helping you love your body; your body helping him love his.

This is heaven: flowers surprising you with their fragrant hellos. No words need be exchanged.

This is heaven: not needing flowers. Rather gather up your lover's smiles than ever-blooming blooms. His smiles are highly nutritious and low in calories—you can munch on them any time you like. Sunflower seeds don't taste as good; not as much hard wisdom in them, I guess.

This is heaven: his mouth addressing your needs; his glorious, well-formed, smooth, wet, animal tongue seeking out your vulnerabilities. His prey, your prey; his lust, your supper. As his tongue zeros in between your legs, you do not aim to please. You move in for the kill: pleasure. His body thanks you. Your body thanks him.

"This is heaven," I tell the young man in my bed, Mr. Dante Algieri, and leave it at that. Who needs words when you have body language ready to make things so beautifully clear?

I recall sex wasn't always like this. I can't say it was Hell, but was it Heaven? No! Not being able to tell the difference between being awake (turned on) and being asleep (turned off) is a really bad place to be. I was asleep for four and a half years and didn't even know it. I couldn't tell the difference between a kiss and a call for help. I could have been drugged, I was so compliant, real patient-like, terrified my old lover, Dr. Guido Cotroni, would leave me and then what? Who would take care of Sleeping Beauty? Who would keep her tranquillized? Wash her face and do her hair? Not that the 40-year-old did these things for me, but I did use the hair stylist he suggested, the shampoo he suggested, the nail polish he asked for; I made myself in his image and he was grateful, as I am now grateful. Grateful, he took care of everything, so I could sleep and keep myself clean and virginal. Grateful he was too busy to become involved; grateful too that he had a wife and children. Thank God, he was too polite to wake me up. Too prudish to lick me to orgasm.

This is heaven: a man and a woman posed to love each other, any which way, upside down, inside out. 69 is my favourite position.

A man can kiss a woman and no damage is done. A man can fuck a woman and keep her fresh and virginal but he can't bring his lips to her cunt, eat pussy, and keep her unmoved; doing it, a man makes her into a woman—his woman. That's why a woman can devirginize another woman. Penetration isn't the aim of the exercise. Orgasm is. What is divine in our bodies, isn't in our brains, but in between our legs ...

The question is: What is heaven like (for real)? An absence of work? (What about the rights of workaholics?) Or is heaven an absence of evil? But that precludes an absence of conflict. How can you live without conflict and not be bored? The more I try to imagine what heaven is like, the less I can imagine it! The only time I can imagine it is after an orgasm, or during the act itself; the pleasure is so perfect, the act of 69 so complete, so sisterly, brotherly, so unifying (the whole world is one big happy place!)—the concept of heaven, well, it doesn't seem so ridiculous then.

Is 69 a holy experience?

Of course, it is.

Dante disagrees. "Here, you have a man and a woman, upside down, and they're licking each other (if they weren't horny they probably wouldn't even like the taste). How can this animal act be holy? You can't look at yourself having sex and not laugh. Nor can you wonder what heaven is like and take yourself seriously."

I agree. "Humour requires wit and wit requires intellect and sex requires pure instinct. You could say sex is both sacred and profane, but actually, there is nothing profane about sex—is there? There is certainly nothing shameful or disgusting about it; farting is shameful, well, embarrassing, but you can't say anything like that about sex. Well, yes, sex is funny, but it is holy as well. Is there a word for that?"

"Sacred humour," he suggests.

"No, no, no, no," I say. "Sacred humour is completely different. It's like saying Alice in Wonderland had a hell of a lot of fun, when the poor girl was lost. A road trip can be fun or adventurous, but if you're on a quest to find the meaning of life, then you're on a pilgrimage, if you know what I mean."

He doesn't know what I mean, he says, but he does.

This is heaven: his hand teasing my hand; his leg, teasing my leg; his body: my joy. What's the point of speculating about heaven, when you can have something better? I didn't think I was capable of such pleasure.

This is heaven: being smeared all over your naked body with fresh blackberries (a true gourmet delight). Is this act funny or holy? A banana placed inside a woman's cunt is clearly funny, but berries bring a different dimension to the act of seduction. For one thing blackberry juice looks too much like blood for it to be funny, and for another, it's sticky and messy. (Thank God my young man cleans up my skin so nicely, I never felt as clean.)

"Don't worry about the sheets," he tells me. "I'll wash them for you." Any man will squeeze fresh berries on your naked body and lick you till you cry with beautiful pain, but what man will take the trouble to wash the sheets you lay on? Only a man who loves you will do that, and that is why even this bizarre act ends up being funny and holy, because as soon as you include love in the act of copulation, profane is out, dirty is out. It becomes clean even when you're as dirty as children playing in the mud, making mud pies for the fun of it.

This is heaven: a place where, if there is a God, his veins

would flow with blackberry juice, as would the Goddess at his side, the two would nourish each other. (It seems a shame adults can't feed off each other like that!) Why shouldn't both men and women have the honour of breastfeeding? Wouldn't it be nice to live in a place where men and women can have their nipples sucked and an endless supply of sweet juice or carbonated drink or alcoholic beverage—whatever you like, honey!—would flow out?

This is heaven: a place where a man and woman would retire to bed and have a midnight snack and not worry about dirtying the sheets, the sheets would wash themselves. They would have to, because in heaven, you can't have maids. You don't want social hierarchies in heaven, do you?

This is heaven: not having to answer to anyone. His tongue is seeing to it you can't talk.

This is heaven ... and this time the gates are closed behind me so I can enjoy my privacy. Goodnight.

In the bedroom I might wonder whether heaven is a garden and God is hiding in it, but in the kitchen I do no such thing. In the kitchen I do not wonder whether God is more like the Grand Canyon, a natural wonder, or more like a man or a woman. In the bedroom I might tell my bedmate that the use of the pronoun, He, for God is outmoded. In the Old Testament God says: "I am the Alpha and Omega, the Beginning and the End," suggesting God has no gender. God is an intrinsic part of our universe. (Is the universe?) The symbol  (an A inside an O), short for Alpha and Omega, might be a worthy alternative to the use of the pronoun, He, for God. (Let ΑΩ's will be done!)

A suicidal maniac might suggest God is a four-legged creature, a kind of praying mantis, which needs to be taken out and squashed. When I am *not* in the kitchen, I might consider such an idea a possibility. But, when I am making supper, or baking a gorgeous chocolate almond cake, there is no way in hell that I could believe God is a beast or beastly for that matter. In the kitchen I cannot think bad thoughts. In the bedroom I might opt to confess my sins to my bedmate, but in the kitchen the world is without sin. In the kitchen I accept that God is a sweet mystery waiting to be solved, but not by me. (I'm too busy having fun!)

# Chapter 3

Medieval writers often compared God to a mirror—everything you did was reflected in it. Television has usurped God's role as the Divine Eye.

Asians believe God is Silence; in North America, God is Speech. In North America talk show hosts have become God's favourite spokespersons. They're busy monitoring the nation's seven deadly sins, allowing their celebrity guests to give the nitty-gritty details of who did what to whom.

Turn up the volume, please. The high priestess of American chit-chat is hearing the confession of the Duchess of Devonshire. Will the Duchess' indiscretions/peccadilloes be forgiven? It's up to the viewers. Buy the Duchess' new book and her debts will be cancelled. Celebrities' true confessions come with a price tag. (Eh, that's their souls up for sale!)

Hear enough celebrities' true confessions and you'll be assured your sins are nothing compared to those who peddle their bad habits (and bad jokes) for a living. So you're in the clear—Heaven is yours for the asking.

Everyone I know would like to have a talk show host for a mom. Be careful what you wish for, I tell them. If you have a talk show host for a mother you might be silenced. Carmelite nuns choose not to speak in public, but if you're the daughter of a talk show host you're not given the choice. Your mom is on the air. (Do not disturb!) Everyone has her ear—but you. Her crew hovers around her like spirit guides. Makeup man, hair man, clothes man. Eyes, lips, nose re-touched; hair, thoughts re-assembled. Daughter pushed aside. I should know. My mother is the real McCoy. Her TV show, *Sandra Live*, is ranked *numero uno* in Montréal, Québec.

My mother is real skilled in the art of chit-chat. If I ever run out of something to say, she'll come to my rescue. Or anyone else's. She has a loyal following—like real churchgoers, they tune in once a day and abide by her teachings. Too bad it's just a local show—her flock can't save the world. Oh well, they did save a whale.

The daughter of a talk show host is lower on the social hierarchy than a circus freak—yes, ma'am, lower than the fattest woman on earth who rolled over in bed one day and accidentally killed her husband; lower than the skinniest woman on earth who has to be hooked up to an IV tube and can only appear on TV via satellite; lower too than the tallest woman on earth or a woman with horns. (Female devils are hard to come by.) I tell you, if the daughter of a talk show host hasn't jumped rope more times than anyone else, doesn't have more tattoos than anyone else, or more fingers or hands or legs or heads, if the daughter of a talk show host isn't in the Guinness Book of World Records, she shouldn't even try to get her mother's attention. (Has nothing to crow about!) The daughter of a talk show host is less inspirational than a *defrocked* priest, less interesting than an *unfrocked* stripper and certainly less noteworthy than a death row inmate who admits to bumping off two husbands and a teenage son for the insurance money.

Wanted dead or alive: freaks.

Even those women who make a career out of watching TV talk shows, I hear, don't often pay much attention to their daughters. (Too ordinary—take me!) Daughters should know better than to ask their mothers out to lunch, because they'll be told: "My schedule is fully booked. Let's do it next week." And then next week comes, and it's postponed.

When I was a little girl my mom didn't pay me much attention, and she didn't even have her own TV show back then. Lucky for me she was working in Italy at the time as a foreign correspondent, and Italians love kids (baby idolatry is still practiced in this country), so my imaginary friends and I were well taken care of. If I had had a father, I wouldn't have needed to enter the world of make-believe, nor would I have needed an army of Italian servants to love me to death. But I didn't have one. I was lonely as hell—the proverbial poor little rich girl.

Loneliness weighs a lot. A freshly slaughtered lamb might be easier to carry around than loneliness. No matter how many times you kill it, the fucking beast comes back to life. When you're lonely, your clothes are always stained—even your shoes are full of blood. (It's invisible to the naked eye, but it sure feels like the real thing.) Squish, squash. Wading through a pool of blood is a lot harder than crossing the Atlantic in a luxury liner. I should know—I've done both. When I was six years old, my mother left her job in Italy and returned to Canada (boarded an ocean liner in Naples, we did).

My father was buried at sea. Not his body, mind you. His spirit. I would have liked to have thrown him overboard but I didn't know where he was. Shit!—I didn't know who he was. (Nor did my mom.) Ever since, loneliness has hung round my neck like a freshly slaughtered carcass.

# Chapter 4

On the agenda: lunch with Dr. Guido Cotroni.

On the menu: *Aragosta alla Newburg, Aragosta ai Ferri, Aragosta alla Thermidor*—a lobster festival. On the menu: "I need you, Sophie." A plea to return.

It's always about his needs. His problems. Here he is with a two-timing wife who promises to return and take care of their two little girls, but can't do it now, 'cause she is too busy building nuclear plants in South America (or is it South Africa now?) and besides, there's yet a new man in her life.

No wonder I dozed off. As soon as I met Dante, the word *our* came out of his mouth. *Our* house. *Our* children. *Our* future together. The operative word. Every time he uses the word *our,* it's like an alarm clock goes off!

A waitress interrupts: "What will it be? In *Italiano—s'il vous plaît.*"

The prime minister of Québec might not know it, but you can't get a job in this area of Montréal unless you're well-versed in Verdi's mother tongue. In this part of town restaurant menus are bilingual—French and Italian. No one would ever guess that back in the 1970s newly-arrived unilingual Italian immigrants were taking to the streets, demanding the right to align themselves with the English-speaking minority of the province of Québec. It was not to be. As soon as Québec's National Assembly passed Bill 101 in 1974 *(La Charte de la langue française)* the proud descendants of the once mighty ancient Roman Empire, acquiesced to the will of the people. Speaking French to the French, English to the English and Italian to each other, the community prospered.

Guido tells the waitress: "My friend doesn't speak Italian." And immediately proceeds to order for me.

Then he says: "I have something to show you, Sophie." For a moment, I think it's his divorce papers.

He picks up his briefcase, opens it and pulls out a copy of *Allo Police*, a tabloid. On the front page is a picture of Dante's uncle, Franco Aglieri, in handcuffs.

"The man is dangerous," he tells me. "People fear his name. You don't have to google it. Most of his relatives living in Palermo are members of the Sicilian Mafia Commission. Franco Aglieri owns half of Saint-Léonard, including the building my dental office is in."

"What of it? Dante's parents aren't rich."

"*Gli Inglesi* always think you have to be rich to be in the Mafia. If you're rich, you don't need the Mafia. You have an army of lawyers and accountants at your beck and call. The Aglieris spell trouble."

"Dante could have worked for his uncle," I tell him. "He chose not to."

"Your fiancé has put *il malocchio* on you. You can't see straight. Franco Aglieri has been charged with fraud, abuse of trust and tax evasion. He is alleged to have participated in a system of bid-rigging that saw a cartel of engineering and construction firms obtain public contracts from *la Ville de Montréal* in exchange for political donations. He is slated to testify before the Charbonneau Commission. Doesn't it worry you, Sophie?"

"I can take care of myself," I assure him.

A lecture ensues: as soon as we enter this world, we need someone to help us out. Contrary to popular opinion, we don't grow up and outgrow our dependence on others.

I tell him: "I've been taken care of—nannies, tutors, music teachers, you name them, and I've had them. Now, it's my turn to take care of others."

Another lecture, and this one focuses on the differences between men of honour (Guido?) and men with bad reputations (Dante, or is it the Mafia I'm supposed to be wary of?).

"Ever since I was a little girl I wanted to get married and have a family," I tell him, my hand on his. He looks at it as if it were a gun.

And to think at one time the sound of his voice, his sighs, his ambitions and half-hearted affection kept me up all night. Didn't I realize how self-centred and self-involved he was? With him, it was always a question of what was "his" and what was "mine"—his car, my car; his pain, my pain.

Luckily, it took just one look to discover Dante across the crowded room, discovering me, and I was hooked. Love-at-first-sight has an animal feel to it. It's all about guts. And guts, like grace, is a gift from God.

The speed of Dante's love startled me. The speed of mine delighted him. The word *our* casts a magic spell.

Dinner at the Aglieris is a noisy affair. Everyone talks at the same time. Everyone is opinionated and how.

Lina, Dante's sister, insists: "You can't be a Buddhist and an Italian. You have to choose between the two."

Dante's older brother, Michele, a Buddhist and a vegetarian, doesn't agree. No creature should be sacrificed for another, he says, passing up his father's home-cured prosciutto.

His father barks back that, when his grandparents were growing up in Southern Italy, meat was a delicacy. Only the rich could afford to eat as much meat as they liked.

The Buddhist fills his plate with olives and roasted peppers and sun-dried tomatoes and cuts himself a thick slab of country-style bread and makes another attempt to convince his family that Buddhism is the perfect way of coming to terms with life.

If you're born rich—no problem, Lina shouts, unimpressed with her brother's rhetoric, but if you're born poor, like they were, then they had it coming? Grin and bear it.

Life is suffering, her brother, the vegetarian, replies, but you can free yourself. That's the challenge, he insists. Do it right and next time, you'll be rewarded.

Don't step on the ants, eh bad karma, says the other, but child labour, who gives a fuck?

To make the world a better place, you have to end sorrow, Michele argues. And to end sorrow you have to follow Buddhism's Eightfold Path.

I find myself reciting *The Eightfold Path*:

*right opinions,*
*right intentions,*
*right speech,*
*right conduct,*
*right livelihood,*
*right effort,*
*right mindfulness,*
*right concentration.*

"Are you a Buddhist?" someone asks.

"I don't follow any religion," I reply. "I wasn't baptized or anything. My mother saw to that."

"That's it," Lina says. "Religion is not something you choose. It's not a garment you can put on or off. You're born into it."

"Catholics are good at forgiving," I suggest.

"Good at vendettas too," snaps the vegetarian. "The Mafia and the culture of forgiveness don't mix well."

Dante's annoyed. Can't they ever have a conversation without bringing up the Mafia? he asks. It's bad enough the American media obsesses over it, making everyone think that anyone who is Italian is a Mafioso. If Italians are poor, they're no good, and if they're rich, they're no good either, because they got rich doing something bad, really bad. The media is out to get Italians. Why, he's not sure.

"No one's Italian here," says his brother, Michele. "When is the last time any of us spoke Italian in this house? If you don't speak the language, you can't make any claims on being a son or daughter of Italy. And even if you did speak the language, what has the Italian culture got to do with us? It's as good as dead. Our grandparents, first generation Italian-Canadians, had links to the old country but we don't."

"*State zitta*," the mother tells him. "You just ate lasagna and you claim you're not Italian?"

"*Oyee* ma, you eat Chinese, you Chinese?"

The question is ignored.

Dante's father offers me yet another glass of his homemade wine. Don't I like it?

Dante's sister insists I try her home-cured dried, spicy sausage, nicely vacuum-packed.

"*Ora si mangia. Mangia, mangia*!" Dante's mother shouts, as if food were the magic ingredient—Holy Communion. Eat up and peace be with you ...

Waiting for the next course of Dante's mamma's home cooking—waiting for a double espresso, waiting for the men to finish their game of *scopa*, waiting for the women to return to their seats (everyone's helping cleaning up, a prelude to the next course, even *la ragazza inglese*), Dante's sister, Lina, out of the blue, tells me that her parents' restaurant is not doing well. The bank might call in the loan. And why? Because their uncle, who is part owner of their restaurant, has been linked to the Mob.

Dante's mother tells her to keep quiet, but Lina dismisses her objections. "*É famiglia*," she says.

Why hadn't Dante said something?

"I didn't want to worry you," he tells me. "Besides, in this country everyone is convinced Italians are crooks. If Italians are poor, we deserve it, we're *i cafoni*, country hicks, and if we're rich, we're still *i cafoni*, but with Mafia connections."

"Sophie, our uncle is no crook," Lina assures me.

"Who loves a crook?" asks Dante.

"Another crook," I answer.

"You lie a lot, Sophie."

"Keeping secrets (don't call it lying!) is essential to staying alive."

"Keep hiding yourself, Sophie, and you'll disappear."

"Either one carries a gun for protection, or one uses one's wit," I tell him.

Power comes in many forms. Sometimes it comes disguised in a business suit. Wall Street gangs hurt more people in one day than street gangs do in a year. The phone is as powerful as a gun. With one phone call my mother landed a colleague's son a position at a prestigious law firm. The man's son objected to her intervention, but he took the job anyway.

"Our uncle is ruthless," Lina says, "but he wouldn't resort to blackmail or arson."

"The man's a crook, but he ain't no monster," Michele says. Or did he say "mobster?"

Waving a spatula Dante's mother says: "*Basta*. Take out the *tiramisu* and let's have dessert. Let's not say another word about this—*capisci*."

Dante's dad refuses to get involved in the argument. "*Tutto passa*," he tells the group. Like, "*i dolci*" are coming. Better finish up *i formaggi e frutta*. (That's what counts!)

Because of their Catholic heritage, Italians are naturally optimistic. Eat up and you'll feel better.

# Chapter 5

Objects in space are far apart. You don't see the sun and the moon crashing into each other. Why then can't Heaven and Hell keep their distance? One moment you're having the time of your life and the next you're in trouble.

The hospital window is open, but much good it does—it's hot. I can't breathe.

Guido's grandfather lies in a diabetic coma. His face is drained of colour, of ambition, of the will to live. The doctors don't expect the 92-year-old to make it through the night.

A priest, a kid fresh out of seminary school, gives the Last Rites. Everyone knows the prayers, except me. I shouldn't be here. I am not a member of the family, but Guido insisted ... I look to the window for comfort.

Legend has it that there are billions of angels watching over us, one angel for each star. Jews, Christians and Muslims believe in the existence of angels. Buddhists and Taoists make reference to them in their sacred writings.

Ancient Greeks and Romans prayed to angels, put their trust in them. Can I? My brain says, yes. My gut says, yes. But I don't see any angels hovering about. Plenty of tears though.

I walk out of the hospital room and look for a bigger window with a better view. The skyscrapers seem to rise out of the ground like ancient Egyptian obelisks inscribed with hieroglyphics. (Wisdom-to-go.)

According to the Egyptian *Book of the Dead*, when the God of the Afterlife, Osiris, met the newly deceased at the pearly gates, they were expected to say:

*Hail to you Lord of Justice,*
*I have not done falsehood*
*I have not deprived the orphan of his property*
*I have not done what the Gods detest*
*I have not caused pain*
*I have not caused hunger*
*I have not made to weep*
*I have not killed*
*I have not made suffering for anyone*
*I am pure pure pure*

Osiris was a God of Judgement. If the newly deceased weren't pure, if they couldn't recite the negative confession and mean it, they couldn't enter the Otherworld. But if they had led a good life Osiris would allow their "*ba*" or "soul" to live there for the next 3,000 years.

Guido takes my hand, wanting to comfort me, even though it's he who needs comforting. I didn't know his grandfather very well. He sat at the dinner table, always at the same place, always in the same dark blue suit. He rarely said a word. Sometimes, at the end of a meal, he'd play a tune on his accordion, but most of the time he would sit motionless and uninvolved. But then everyone spoke English around the table, and he didn't understand the language. I wish I could now ask his forgiveness for having been part of the conspiracy to shut him out, but it's too late.

Guido puts his arm around my shoulder, and despite his mother's look of disapproval, keeps it there. Suddenly I remember why I was so taken with him. Even here, squeezed between two old chairs, two sad hospital chairs, I feel safe. You don't need religion or a belief in the afterlife to feel safe. You just need someone to love you.

# Chapter 6

Devotees of *Sandra Live* had asked for a show on ADCs—After-Death Contacts. Her devotees didn't have to worry about their prayers not being answered. Her staff made sure the telephone lines were always open. For them. Not for me though. I can't get within earshot of the star of the show. Can't I see my mom's busy? (Never mind she always is.)

The host starts the show rolling: 47 per cent of widows and widowers have communicated with their dead partner (no joke); 1 out of 6 has seen his or her partner's ghost. A Freud look-a-like, a Dr. Somebody, readily admits reports of the bereaved seeing loved ones after they pass away are common, and he would go so far as to call the events normal, part of a healthy grieving process. But don't get him wrong. He doesn't believe the visitations are proof of anything. He regards the apparitions as products of the subconscious rather than actual contacts from the dead. Stress can trigger hallucinations, and an apparition is a hallucination, except it is seen when you are awake, rather than in a dream state.

Guest No. 1 is quick to disagree. It wasn't a figment of his imagination, he says. He did see his wife at the foot of his bed. She looked perfectly real. She didn't speak to him, but she communicated her thoughts telepathically. "I'm okay," she told him. And then, before he could stop her, she walked towards the wall and melted into it.

The host is amazed and sides with the widower. No one knows what happens after one dies, she says. Medical experts don't know, theologians and philosophers don't have a clue either. But not to worry. Listen to your gut—it tells you death is just another stage of existence, lived on another plane or in another dimension. And on to the next guest ... but this one can't perform on cue (tears get in the way). The poor woman tells her sad tale: her five-year-old was killed in a car accident a few days after her grandmother died. Prior to the little girl's death she complained her dead grandmother was begging her to come and live with her in heaven.

The host asks for a break ... She walks off the set. Her crew and I follow. Off camera, she reprimands her assistants. Why had this sad little woman been invited to sit on the panel? Hadn't she made it plain? She wanted uplifting stories.

Explanations are given, a number of staff are on holidays, and the head researcher is on maternity leave.

Despite the staff's objections—can't I see my mother's busy? Besides, they fucked up, do I want to too? I confront my mother right then and there, and tell her I am getting married.

"I knew your dentist would come around," she says.

"It's not the dentist."

"Who then?"

I could tell her he's an architect. She'd like that. She's such a snob.

"He's a dance instructor," I say.

"Ballet?"

"Ballroom."

The mother of all mothers doesn't verbalize her disappointment. Her smile, her intelligence, her grace, her thoughts impress everyone—even me; too bad they suppress my own. She dominates the area like a host of daffodils, which is to say she does it naturally, without malice. She's wonderfully competent, nice even, so I know I am in the wrong here, but gee, I can't help being a little girl starving for ... What it is, I'm not quite sure.

On the store counter: mounds of designer label wedding dresses my mother picked out for me—a *Vera Wang*, a *Stella*, a *Jasmine* and a *Marchesa*.

"Which one do you like the best?" she asks, taking out her wallet.

"I don't need a wedding dress. I have one. I showed it to you."

"Sophie, you're not going to wear that old thing."

"That old thing is an original *Charles James*."

"You bought it in a thrift shop!"

"One can find vintage clothing anywhere, even at the Salvation Army. One has to know what to look for."

"Why, Sophie, do you want to wear someone else's hand-me-down?"

"I don't see the point in buying an expensive dress that I will wear once. Once! Honestly, I don't enjoy buying stuff. Shop till you drop? What for? I can go on eBay and find exactly what I need, when I need it, for a tenth of the price. I don't need a car. I can bike. I take no pride in owning stuff. I am *not* what I wear. I am *not* what I do. Are you surprised?"

"Why would I be surprised? You espouse the views of your generation. The Millennials. You believe, as do your friends, that life is for living. I don't object to that. Why should anyone work their ass off? Certainly not for a pay cheque. The problem is that you and your friends assume, wrongly assume, that what we now have in this beautiful, freedom-loving, democratic country of ours can be maintained without a fight. You have no ambition. No will to protest. It was my generation who gave women a voice. It was my generation who insisted on redefining what it means to be happy ... *I think therefore I am*? No way! A cat or dog can think. What differentiates us from our animal cousins is our willingness to act. To go beyond our biological needs. Growing up I vowed I would not be like my mother. She spent her whole life moping around the house, yearning for babies, and the right to be loved by my father, who was not all that loving. I understood that if I wanted to have value, survive in this heartless world of ours, I had to make a name for myself. I had to be of service."

"I am not the daughter you should have had. I don't share your need to excel. It sounds childish, I know it, but growing up, I just wanted to fit in. Be like everybody else. Have a mother and a father. I suppose if I had had lots of sisters, I might have had enough of hand-me-downs, but I didn't. You always bought me more clothes than I needed, or wanted!"

"Any other daughter would be grateful to have her wedding dress paid in full, but not you!"

I should say I'm sorry, but I don't.

"Other children asked Santa for Barbie dolls," she says, "but you always insisted on the one thing I couldn't give you."

"Which was?"

"A sister."

My mother still can't forgive me for making a demand she couldn't fulfil, and vice versa.

Ever since I watched the sun and the moon undress the sky of its colour, ever since I could tell the difference between a "him" and a "her," ever since I could define the line between a "me" and a "you" and protect myself accordingly, I longed for a sister. Ever since I understood I was an accident (or, as mother would say, a surprise), ever since I knew I came into the world dangling on a string, a joker *sans* joke, ever since I sensed the world is teeming with lonesome travellers and pleasure-seekers *sans* purpose, I longed for a sister. Ever since I was singled out and ostracized because my eyes were the wrong colour (or was it my hair?), ever since I was left out in the cold, refused membership in a club or been un-invited to a party, I longed for a sister to comfort me, tell me an injustice had been done—I was good enough. Ever since I managed to override feelings of self-pity and betrayal, ever since I managed to entertain friends and lovers, foolishly smiling, ever since the spectacle (all smiles) guaranteed success (yes, I could fit in!), I wished for a sister, a blood relative, who accepted me as I was—smiles, or no smiles. Ever since I understood the medicinal effects wild flowers had on moods, I understood I could never be healed no matter how many floral beauties haunted my house and garden. Ever since I found myself poisoned, having drunk too much star light or moon shine (who knows what is what?), I longed for a sister to help me out, erase the sad feelings. Ever since I could read, ever since I could understand which fables were true and which were wishful thinking, ever since I could right wrongs and choose not to do so, ever since I could take in my image in the mirror and be dissatisfied, I longed for a sister, a co-conspirator. (My dear, you're not alone, I am like you!) Ever since my body grew limbs, organs, consciousness, that's it—ever since that first cell divided in my mother's womb, yes, ever since then, I longed for a sister. Ever since, oh my God, God gave birth to $H_2O$, I longed for a sister and if I didn't, I couldn't (wasn't made flesh yet). Yes, ever since I took a sip of water and cherished it because I was thirsty, I was in need of a sister. Ever since my primal needs were taken care of, I longed to have a sister to love me. Oh my God, yes, ever since my eyes took in the sun and the moon, which is to say ever since I can remember, I wanted a sister.

# Chapter 7

If one had a "Time Machine," one could travel back in time, but none exist, so if one wants to step back in time, a museum or antique shop will have to do.

Guido thinks he can turn back the clock. He enters the antique shop I work in bearing gifts—flowers and a box of chocolates filled with poisoned promises.

"Marry me," he says. "I love you," he says. He says all the things I would have liked to have heard in the past, but now leave me cold. A lecture ensues about the differences between love and lust, between penniless young men (like Dante) and older ones who can provide comfort and security (like himself, I gather).

"Don't be reckless," he says. Like, don't marry for love, marry for money?

"Everything I have, I had to fight for," he says. He put himself through university, working two part-time jobs. Now, his dental practice is thriving and he owns a big house in Saint-Léonard, but is he happy? He needs the big house to remind himself he is a success. He feels like a general who was ordered to seize the property.

Everything about Guido makes me think of war; even his affection for me has an overbearing militaristic feel to it. He tries too hard to conquer. I don't want to be conquered. I am shamelessly in love with the enemy.

The general is in pain, and it's definitely my fault. Dante never blamed me for anything.

I think of Dante and my body is wet with anticipation. Because he and I made love on the Queen Anne-style carved mahogany double settee, the shop is filled with his sweet, harsh scent. Everywhere I turn I get a whiff of it.

"What is it you want?" Guido asks.

"I want to be happy."

"North Americans believe the pursuit of happiness is their birthright. Immigrants don't fool themselves. They know, if you make happiness the point of your life, you'll get disappointed. Living in someone else's country is like buying a used car, if you could do better, you would."

Something tells me, prepare yourself, Sophie. Something has happened. It's my gut speaking. A bad sign ... Exiting out of the *Jean-Talon* Metro Station, I notice an armed security guard stationed in front of the *Casa d'Italia*. This is highly irregular. The Art Deco building, an Italian community centre, dating back to the 1930s, houses a wealth of documents and archival photos, but it has nothing of material value. Why, the guard? Are the directors of the *Casa* preparing for a gala event for a political head of state. Or is Franco Aglieri, who recently donated 50,000 dollars to the *Casa*, expected to make his appearance? Walking west, towards the church of *La Madonna della Difesa,* everywhere I turn I hear the damn sound of sirens. Cops everywhere. *La Petite-Italie* looks like an urban war zone. I follow the crowd out of *Marché Jean-Talon* and turn the corner, and there on *boulevard Saint-Laurent*—Oh my God!—Dante's family restaurant, *Chez Nina*, is up in flames. The area is so full of smoke, I can't get close to it.

I see a man (it can't be Dante's uncle?) staggering towards his car, his hands covered with blood. I hug the wall for support.

Someone in the crowd tells me: "There was an explosion just before the fire started. It sounded like a plane taking off: *boom*, *boom*, *boom*, one after the other. I bet the Mafia had a hand in this."

The word, Mafia, is on everyone's lips. It comes up over and over again, like a chant in a black mass. It might very well be the name of the new anti-Christ. Say "*mon Dieu*" on this island and someone will not know what it means. Say, Mafia, and everyone does.

How can something as destructive as a fire be beautiful? Are the fires in Hell beautiful? Can the fires in Hell be put out? And if they can be, are tears used? Enough around here to do the job.

Insurance investigators descend on the Aglieris' restaurant. Dante's father shows them around, offering his version of events. The fire was so intense and moved so quickly, he tells them, that he had no time to take any of his belongings. His office was gutted. Luckily, the fire was contained quickly and no one was hurt. Most of the damage to the area was caused by the water the firemen used to put out the flames.

Waitresses are lined up; busboys interviewed. One question follows another. Questions: hooks. Answers: the big catch of the day. A promotion. Front page coverage ... Police uncover Mafia ring to defraud the public. (Watch out, folks, your *veal scaloppine* could be made from pork.) End of organized crime and the beginning of a "Just Society." And all because the Aglieris were ready to talk, confess to arson, or at least, to participating in the underground economy.

I had been on my mother's production company payroll for years and no one asked me to produce proof thereof. When the upper classes up their expenses, make use of tax loopholes created for and by their cronies, they're applauded for their business savvy; when busboys and waitresses pocket a little change, apocalypse is a-coming.

Dante's father offers the insurance investigators coffee, cappuccino, espresso—take your pick. If he's upset, he doesn't show it.

"It will take a couple of weeks before a decision is made on your claim," the younger of the two insurance investigators, an Italian, tells Dante's father, enjoying a second slice of cake and a tall espresso. If it were up to him, they'd have had a cheque in the mail yesterday. But they had to be 100 per cent sure that they weren't dealing with insurance fraud here. Hadn't he recently increased his insurance coverage?

"So did every other businessman on this street."

"That's just it," says the investigator. "If your insurance

claim comes through, you could renovate this place and make a mint. Didn't your bank recently turn you down for a loan, Mr. Aglieri?"

"I live on the second floor of this building. Would I set fire to my own house?" he replies, hurt.

"Every fire has to be investigated," the Italian tells him. Nothing personal.

As soon as the two men leave, the Aglieris discuss their options. I could be at a board meeting. No one is hysterical or out of control, except *l'inglese*—me! I'm supposed to accept that under the circumstances the wedding has to be postponed.

Suddenly it is winter and I am in Venice. A funeral cortège makes its way down the Grand Canal.

"There's Daddy," a little girl cries out. Laid out on the four-poster gilded barge, heavily draped in black, is the body of the man I love.

And then I wake up.

Kissing dispels anxiety better than any drug. Kissing, the fear of closed spaces, the fear of heights—any phobias you may have—are put to rest. Kissing resolves fights; you can't erase what has been said, but you'd never know it when you're kissing.

Kissing opens the gates to extreme pleasure. Kissing on a park bench is good. Kissing on the beach is good too. (Would have to move to California to understand just how good, good is, but no matter.) Kissing is about the present and cherishing it. (Can't put a kiss away like a letter, or send it off to the future, you have to love it *as is*, now or never!) Kissing on a crowded street corner where chain smokers curse in every which language isn't recommended, nor in a red light district, across a topless bar. But no one will arrest you if you do, so go ahead. Kissing across a big neon ad for Eternity, the perfume, makes me uncomfortable because the girl in the ad is undressed and the city I live in is cold (spring no exception). Kissing in a casino where grown-ups gamble away their fortunes is unwholesome, but that's only my opinion. Many do it, and Lady Luck approves.

Kissing in the Tower of Babel, or at the crossroads of Heaven and Hell, wouldn't turn me on, but that's neither here nor there. So I would rather consider this: when you're kissing, that ever-elusive *pot of gold at the end of the rainbow* is yours for the asking.

When you are kissed as I am kissed, your flesh becomes precious—it's your heirloom. Kisses are more valuable than gold or 20-carat blue diamond rings. (And you don't even have to pan in a creek or blow up a mountain to get at them; your partner does all the work for you.) Kissing makes you rich; your future is secured. There's a next generation waiting to be mined (oh hurry up and do it!) and it's all yours, because of a little kiss.

Kissing on top of *Mont-Royal* is a wonderful way to start off a birthday celebration; the Milky Way is more visible on top of a mountain, and its one billion stars can make do as birthday candles. Or then, maybe not. Kissing, it doesn't matter if I am 28 or was 28, and whether God is coming to terms with its own (in)finite nature. Kissing, this birthday girl doesn't wonder how old God is or what sex God identifies with or if He's married. Kissing, the nature of the universe or how a Creator can be created without a bride and a bridegroom having stolen a few kisses prior to the Big Day (or Big Bang) is not at issue. Kissing, participating in the ancient skin ritual, life is its own reward.

Kissing relieves tension. Kissing increases IQ scores. Kissing makes God love you and so I put my crooked lips on his beautiful ones.

At the moment conversation does not interest me; what a waste—words. I rather bring his lips to mine than introduce ideas into the room.

"Is it me or my body you're after?" Dante wants to know.

"Your body," I say, jokingly.

"Wrong answer," he says.

He turns on his laptop; a tango, I don't recognize, screeches out.

"Ballroom dancing is not my thing," I remind him.

"It's not mine either," he says. "I prefer the Argentine tango. It's less restrictive. There are no basic steps. You have to *feel* the dance. Essentially you are walking with your partner, close together, ankles and knees brushing as one leg passes the other. The music has a clear, repetitive beat. Lyricists have written hundreds of songs for the tango. '*Adios Pampa Mia*' is one of the most famous. Listen to the lyrics: '*Goodbye, my pampa. I'm leaving for strange lands. If we don't see each other again, I want you to know that in my departure I leave my life. Goodbye, roads that I have travelled; goodbye roads that I have dreamed on. One day I will return to your soil, my beloved land. My soul will escape like a dove up into the sky. Goodbye, I'm leaving.*'"

"The tango makes me sad," I tell him. "It reminds me of my childhood. Back then I was often teased and taunted and made fun of because I did not have a father. Others may not have had fathers living at home with them, but they knew who they were. I did not have a clue. No name. No photo. Nothing. My mother dismissed my questions. Why, why, why should I care about who my father was—when I had it all? I had her. I lived in a big house in Westmount. I imagined one day my father would show up, and then I would be like everyone else—happy. I wouldn't feel worthless, like I was a copy of someone else, a clone made in a petri dish. In high school I simply told my classmates that my father was dead and then I was accepted. I was invited to parties and ski trips and I pretended I was normal, and I liked it. I don't want to feel the pain, the nostalgia, the anxiety of distances, and the longing to return home, because I am exactly where I want to be—I'm with you. I'm happy."

"You're one of a kind, Sophie. A divine woman ... The tango contains the promise of happiness. The hope for a better life. The tango was created by and for immigrants. You can't immigrate, and be a pessimist. Or a coward. When you tango, you exchange one country for another, fusing cultures. The tango honours the journey; the odyssey. The maze. When you tango, you believe the best is yet to come."

Try as I might, I can't do it.

"Pretend we're in Buenos Aires," he says. "The year is 1910. I'm a migrant worker and you're a local girl from a good family. You can't speak Italian and I can't speak Spanish, but it doesn't matter. When you tango there are no social barriers. Everything is possible. When you tango, you stand tall. Arch your back. Come on, Sophie, show off!"

Me show off? That's like asking a marathon champion and a woman with a limp (me!) to trade places.

"Sophie, if anyone thinks they're it, it's you! You wear old rags and think it great fun. An Italian would never wear second-hand clothing. Italians are insecure, they always have to make *la bella figura*, but the English don't give a fuck."

"I'm Italian," I assure him. "Well, half Italian anyway. My father was a *bone fide* Roman. Well, he could easily have been. Most of the men my mother worked with (and had affairs with) were born in Rome."

"I doubt your dad was Italian," he says.

And why not?

"You don't look Italian. You don't speak Italian. And you can't dance! Besides, if you were Italian, you wouldn't want to marry me. Italian girls are social climbers. They're materialistic and terribly old-fashioned. They look for men who can keep them in style. And if they can't, they're tossed out. My cousins expect to make *good* marriages. Growing up, they went to private schools; spent their summers in their father's villa in Palermo. I was asked to tag along, but the last thing I wanted was their pity. I could have worked as an architect for my uncle's construction company, but I didn't want to build structures that are functional and cheap. What interests me is green building sustainable design. That's what I specialized in. But buildings that use solar energy and recycled materials cost more; investors don't want to bear the expense. And so now I am not working in my field. An Italian girl would never consider marriage to someone who waits tables. You should have stayed with Guido. He's rich and I'm not."

Assurances I would rather sit on the floor with someone I love than sit on a genuine Italian leather sofa with someone I don't care about, fall on deaf ears. But enough talk.

I take off my little black dress (a vintage *Dior*!), revealing a whale-boned corset (it cost a small fortune), but the Victorian undergarment draws no oohs and aahs.

I kiss my husband-to-be, but he does not kiss me back. He insists on continuing the dance lesson, despite my obvious lack of interest.

I plead for a break. I find the tango, *Se Dice de Mi*, on YouTube and tease him with the words: "*It's said about me that I am ugly. That I walk bowlegged like a gangster, and my mouth is like a mail box. My waistline is gone.*"

Dante teases me: "*But the ugliness that God gave you, many envy. They haven't seen you in a nightgown. You have the skin of a doll.*"

"Do I?"

"You asked me to teach you to tango, Sophie. And I will! You can't do it unless you understand what it's about."

He takes a piece of chalk and draws a circle on the floor, and then draws another circle. 

"The innermost circle," he says, "represents the place of one's birth; the other circle, the country one immigrates to. What's important can't be found inside the first or the second circle. What's important lies beyond the two circles. When you tango, you reach that place. It contains the world. The cosmos. The theory of everything."

I agree—the tango does away with borders. The world is at our fingertips. Well, it should be, and it is, when I'm on the internet, but on the dance floor—no way. Try as I might, I can't learn the steps! I'm helpless and hopeless.

"Under the circumstances I should leave?" I ask.

"Leave and I will die—figuratively speaking."

I undress and who knows what will happen? This is heaven.

I'm at the Aglieris having supper. "Why don't you eat with us?" I ask Dante. "You love *cannelloni*."

"In the Otherworld, where I come from," he says, "we don't eat. Our pleasure comes from watching you eat."

And then I wake up.

# Chapter 8

The crucifix reeks of innocence, of hope—good things come to those who wait. (Heaven is for real!) Look at a crucifix when you're unhappy and it comforts you. (You're not alone! You have a friend in Jesus.) Look at it on your wedding day and the Light pouring out can blind you ... Best to focus on the face of your groom. His smile can help you forget man's cruelty to man; 2,000 years of violence can't compete with this moment.

Like a nun ready to give herself up to a beautiful idea, I give myself up to the groom. He says: "I do," and I say: "I do," and the history of the world, my world, our world, changes.

I want to tell him (but I don't): "Use my love as an antidote against pain. Use my love as you would use an opiate. Let it dull sorrow. Let it help you sleep better. Let it help you rise and shine, and see the world through rose-coloured glasses. Let my love tease you—laughter is the best medicine. Use my love as I will use your love. Love is my drug of choice, as it was Jesus'. Love wishes away suffering. In love: power—the power to heal. In love, the miracle of life everlasting. Love me and I will serve you. (No kidding!) In love, the joy of servitude. In love, the possibility of a pain-free existence. (Love adds to the world's stockpile of all-natural opiates.) Love me and I will be healed (if not today, then tomorrow). Love me and I will become a miracle worker. Love me and heaven is close by, and if it isn't, I'll do my best to fool you into thinking it is. In love, the miracle of self-deception. In love, the miracle of denial. In love: merriment."

I tell my husband (there I said it, husband!): "Love me and I will love you. Don't love me and I will still love you."

The crucifix does not tell a sad tale. That's why it can hang in a church during a wedding ceremony. The crucifix promises happily ever after to anyone who asks.

The weather changes, so do moods. I should be happy. The wedding reception at the Ritz-Carlton Hotel, compliments of my mother's production company, *The Big Bad Wolfe*, couldn't be better. No expense was spared. The flowers, the food and the service—top quality. Except my daddy's not here; daddy has been missing for a long time now. He could be in the Otherworld for all I know.

I don't know why I started thinking about my dad, the unholy ghost, though I suspect watching my mother hovering around Michele may have had something to do with it. She can't let up, even at my wedding. She's an expert at seducing young men; disillusioned intellectuals are her specialty. The 38-year-old doesn't have a chance.

By the end of the evening, he'll be in her bed. In her eyes feminism gave women permission to be as promiscuous as men. She discards them faster than pantyhose. Out they go. Time to move on to the next idea. Young men arouse more than her libido; it's their ideas that enthral her, and just as fast bore her. She could never understand my loyalty to Guido; she chided me, discouraged me and begged me to try out other men. What was I doing with a man nearly a dozen years my senior, standing by him like an old Italian wife, forever loyal and available? If I wanted the good life, I should chase after men my own age. Vitality ages fast in men, she lectured. Women's skin ages faster than men's, that's true, but their vitality remains the same. That's why she hungered for younger men—it was their vitality that she was after—it matched her own. When I told her about Dante she was delighted. "Finally, you've found a man who will wake you up," she said. The fact that he did, proved her theory. And so it could mean Mother Knows Best.

But here she is joking, flirting, intellectualizing with my husband's older brother, Michele, and I don't like it much. I don't want him to be hurt. I approach the pair, wanting to separate them, wanting to spare him the discomfort of an affair with my mother. I have seen dozens of men just like him toyed with, dismissed and demoted; yes, demoted. Mother has a Midas touch in reverse—each man she touches suffers the consequences. It isn't that she is vindictive or that she deliberately sets up to break their hearts or damage their careers; on the contrary, there seems no rhyme or reason why it should happen. But it always does. After she has had her fill of them, she goes on to greener pastures, but the men have problems replacing her. (She's unique, a phenomenon.) Unsatisfied, their lives fall apart. The one person she didn't manage to hurt was my father. He hadn't been around long enough.

I approach the two, lifting my long gown (a French import, mother's choice) and I do my best to come between the two lovebirds, deep in conversation about the Mafia. (What else?)

Michele is giving my mother a short history of the Mafia in North America. (She's all ears.) He argues that Prohibition brought in organized crime. Had the United States government not banned the sale of liquor in the 1920s, no one would ever have come to hear of the Mafia.

"Prohibition had a hidden agenda," he says. "By getting rid of the alcohol, the government hoped to get rid of the Wops."

Mother's confused. It doesn't often happen she can't follow someone's line of thinking.

"At the turn of the 20th century Italians were the most hated immigrant group in the country," Michele says. "They were known as *white niggers.* They would work for next to nothing, and volunteer for dangerous jobs, just so they could send their families back home an extra buck. In New Orleans, the new arrivals, Sicilians for the most part, operated their own businesses and did exceptionally well. This upset the locals. Other immigrant groups, like the Danes and the Dutch, knew their place, it took decades for them to get a foothold in society, and here was this group of Pope-loving nobodies managing to get a big slice of the American pie. New Orleaners decided there was no way in hell Italians could get rich unless they were involved in criminal activities. When the city's chief of police was murdered in 1891 they immediately pinned the crime on a group of Italians, alleged Mafiosos. The men were convicted, tried and found innocent. A mob took over the courthouse and just before the Italians were released, they were either hung, shot or clubbed to death. Italians have the honour—dishonour—of being part of the largest mass lynching in American history. This set in motion a chain of events. Even though there was no evidence for it Americans decided that Italians had a predisposition to crime. The country was unwilling to accommodate the tired, poor and huddled masses of Southern Italy (those Mafia thugs!), but as they couldn't close their borders to them, they decided to pass laws, making the country unattractive to those who could easily and quickly move up the ranks and join the upper-middle classes. Legislators passed Prohibition laws, hoping to drive wine-loving Italians out of the country. At that time it was acceptable to drink a cocktail before or after a meal, but only winos (and Italians!) mixed food and drink. The Prohibition laws didn't succeed in motivating Italians to return home, nor did it stop others from coming to the Land of Milk and Honey. Italians have a knack for making the best of a bad situation."

Suddenly Mother sees the light. She agrees with everything Michele says. His conspiracy theory is right on the money. Yes, yes, yes, the United States government did everything in its power to get rid of Italians whose (alleged) criminal activities made them rich. It couldn't very well have shipped them back home; well, it had done it to the Chinese, but they were smaller in number. Italians were the largest immigrant group at the time—over three million had passed through Ellis Island. So the legislators banned the drinking of wine at the dinner table and everywhere else, expecting a large exodus of Italians, but it didn't happen. Italians, being a resourceful lot, not only continued to make their own wine and liquors (indifferent to government policy), they also applauded those who sold alcohol under the table.

My mother sees no reason to challenge Michele's conspiracy theory; on the contrary, she parrots his views, mirrors his contempt and disgust with the United States government. The speed at which she can pick up on the other's point of view is incredible. She knows how to empathize. That's why she is so successful. Actually, she does one better. She becomes the person you want her to be. That's her strategy. She can't do it with me though. That's what bothers her. She can swindle anyone, be anyone, except be my mom.

"Is your uncle, Franco Aglieri, involved in the Mafia?" my mother asks Michele, point blank.

"Of course not," he tells her, but he does know someone in the Mafia who owns a poultry truck. "Imagine what you can hide in the cavity of a dead chicken!"

Now she won't let go of him. She's found a story! Her story. She's always on the lookout for new material. Like a rare book collector she has a ferocious appetite for that unique find.

Damn it, I didn't want to hear about the Mafia at my wedding. A bad omen. I want to erase the conversation from the record. It didn't happen. This isn't another story conference she's having with her underlings (ask and thou shalt be given!). This is my wedding.

The host of *Sandra Live* unbuttons her blouse—just

enough to reveal a beautiful pair of manufactured boobs, both the same size (no bra). Thank God Dante's parents can't see this. Only Michele is here and he'll see them anyway soon enough.

"Cat got your tongue?" she says to me. "Speak up."

Dare I say what's on my mind? It's her fault I didn't have a dad to walk me down the aisle. It's her fault I don't have a sister. My father might have sired dozens of children, but I'll never meet them.

Mother says: Everyone loves a good Mafia story. No one loves the Hells Angels, The Rock Machine, The Outlaws or street gangs of any kind, because, well, they're associated with anarchy and shoot-outs, but the Mafia's code of behaviour harks back to them good old days. Nostalgia is in the air. Aging females are nostalgic for a time men didn't dump their older wives for younger ones; aging men are nostalgic for a time they didn't have to pay alimony, and children are nostalgic for two-parent families. You know how it is.

Mother says: In the new corporate America, loyalty to a company doesn't guarantee you much. Capitalism and greed are becoming synonyms, and so, the Mafia family is the new Institution the public looks up to. Now here you expect loyalty; you expect brotherly love to take precedence over anything else. In the Mafia family blood ties count for something. Because Godfather types stay married, pamper their adult kids with gifts, go to church (who goes to church these days?), they are becoming part of folklore. National symbols. You might even say Godfather types are what right-wing America looks to for inspiration. Everyone loves a good Mafia story. The Mafia represents traditional family values, that's why.

Mother says: Never you mind Mafia kingpins order hundreds of hits a year. In the 21st century evil is tolerated. If you can get what you want, when you want it, bully for you. Anti-heroes are in vogue. The Mafia represents the Modern Psyche. This is the first time in human history there are no gods to be afraid of. Everyone's a narcissist; meaning, everyone believes in Heaven, but no one believes in Hell. Heaven is yours for the asking. Even psychopaths have a chance at it. And as for God, He's not dead—the Man's retired. He has been put out to pasture. His assistants are looking after the place. Pagan gods are making a comeback. As are angels.

Mother says: It's the first time in history we live in an amoral world, a world without rules—except for no-smoking signs—(mind you, though, our cars can smoke up as much as they like, babies or no babies around). A world without moral imperatives is the best of all possible worlds. It makes democracy come alive! Anyone can be a celebrity. You don't have to be super smart, super strong, super anything; television allows for broad definitions of what constitutes a special person; saint, sinner—all are loved.

Mother says: Television producers would be willing to pay big money for anyone with intimate connections to the Mafia (wink, wink). The Mafia is a driving force behind insurance fraud (wink, wink). If the Aglieris have a story and want to tell it, there's an audience for it (wink, wink).

Michele is visibly irritated. "After years of being at the

helm of a construction empire, after years of being wined and dined by politicians, after years of being on the board of directors of a hospital and a university, my uncle still has to put up with suspicion he's a Mafioso."

"Your uncle should give his side of the story," my mother says. "He should come on my show."

"It won't change anything," he says. "Everyone is prejudiced. The media most of all."

"The media is not as bad as you think," she insists. "What do we do? We tell stories. Everyone wants their story told. Their sins forgiven. It doesn't matter who is in the confessional. What's important is the camera, not the host. The real challenge for a host is to get people to stop talking! Put a TV camera in the room and even murderers and child pornographers open up. It's as if God were behind the camera, taping the show, and you can't but tell the truth."

"The Mafia's code of silence was broken—not by lawmakers, but by TV show hosts," Michele admits, with expected sarcasm.

My mother agrees: "The ten commandments of good journalism: no. 1, pry & spy, no. 2, pry and spy. I said it before, and I'll say it again—we're a nation of voyeurs. And of blabbermouths."

"A marriage made in heaven," retorts Michele.

"*Sandra Live* is doing a show on the Montreal Mafia," she says.

"Don't you dare!" I say.

"Don't worry, Sophie. I'm producing the show. I'll have artistic control."

"Like hell you will."

"You do what you have to do," she says. An American network has shown interest in her show. It might pick it up and then, who knows? There might be a position open for an assistant director. (Michele studied Communications at Concordia University, didn't he?)

And what about me? Don't I want to get a "good" job? One of her researchers ran off to a nunnery (where else, but to Calcutta, helping out Mother Theresa's do-gooder outfit!). I could fill in for her.

I thank her, but I don't want to get into show business and pay lip service to the big white devil: Greed.

Mom says: But Sophie, you're a married woman now, you need a career.

I tell her: I like what I do, Ma. Ma, I don't want a career. Ma, I don't want to be like you. Ma, don't you get tired of your job? Your fame? I do. (It hovers above me like a poisonous gas. I can never be free of it.) Let go, Ma!

And she does!

The first dance is announced and it's not a tango. It's a slow dance: *Ti voglio bene assai*. Even *The Champion of Left Feet* can manage it.

# Chapter 9

Thank you, Air Canada, for the smooth flight.

It's glorious to have wings; glorious to wake up in the wonderful wee Land of We—*oui, oui, oui*. We made it to the other side of the Atlantic. Our first night as Mr. and Mrs. couldn't have been better. Because I have been married for a good 24 hours, I am better off than I was a day ago, better off than I was 24 days or 24 years ago because then I didn't know I had a guardian angel, and now I am sure of it!!!

I am looking straight at her!!! She's dressed in jeans and a T-shirt. Okay, she is not sitting inside the airplane, but *outside* it, cross-legged on the tip of the left wing. What's her name, I wonder? How old is she? Do her wings match the colour of her skin? Dare I say it?—she hasn't any wings! Okay, I'm not a reliable source. I'm crazy and I'm happy. Or crazy because I am happy. Happy, happy, happy. When you're this happy, it's like you can see and hear and smell better than ever. A dog's sense of smell is 1,000 times better than a man's. And so, when you are happy, you gain what a dog takes for granted. You smell better! And you see better as well. When you're happy, you gain a sixth sense. And a third eye! Be happy and enter the world of the surreal. Be happy and enter the Otherworld. Be happy and do nothing. Happiness is it! (Is it ever!)

Dante isn't convinced happiness, the state of mania, opens your eyes to the spirit world. Dante isn't convinced happiness can lift you out of your body and allow your spirit to walk on water. Dante isn't convinced we're immortals and don't know it. Dante isn't convinced you can graduate from nothing-hood to saint-hood in a matter of minutes. (All you need is the presence of a guardian angel.) Dante isn't convinced miracles are part of everyday life. Nor is he convinced guardian angels go around, sitting cross-legged, on the wings of Boeing 727s, dressed in jeans and T-shirts.

How can one sit inside a Boeing 727 and not think of angels and miracles? I argue. Like, how can 500 tonnes of metal fly? Sure, there's a scientific explanation—(don't have to assume twelve legions of angels must be close by, helping out)—but does the understanding of aerodynamics make the event less of a miracle?

Dante says: It's easier to believe in angels than in God. God is stereotyped, is still seen as a little old man with a beard, but angels are seen as progressive—unisex. Angels are more like aliens from outer space, than spirits from inner space.

I agree. In fact, early Christians believed angels had no wings, and left no footprints. Later on, medieval thinkers agreed angels were non-corporeal (had no flesh, no organs, hence ate no food), were neither male nor female, but because of their superior status were able to assume whatever form they liked. (Shape-shifters!)

Dante says: Angels are popping out everywhere—angel figures adorn upholstery, draperies, bedspreads, wallpaper, anything and everything. Angel knickknacks and decorations are a fast growing market. They're propelling the New Age of consumerism. Everywhere you turn individuals are discarding statues of Madonnas, saints and revolutionary heroes but they're hanging onto their little cherubs. Who needs saints? They're far too human. What we crave for are superhuman individuals with superhuman powers. Batman, Superman, Spawn—all of the comic book super heroes fly. Give a guy wings and he's a superstar.

Dante says: A recent poll found that unicorns, fairies and witches have lost credibility, but not angels. Two thirds of us believe in angels.

"Do you?" I ask.

"It doesn't matter," he says. "The existence of angels can't be proven or disproved. The real question is: If you have a guardian angel, will the world be a better place?"

"I hope so," I answer.

Dante isn't convinced.

Sophie, stop imagining things.

Sophie, no more visions.

Sophie, keep your feet on the ground.

My bridegroom is *my* guardian angel, I decide. (Using the adjective "*my*" sounds so possessive, but he doesn't mind, so why should I?) The man is as handsome as a lion. (I could have said he's as handsome as a movie star, but I've seen ugly creatures born and bred in Hollywood, California. I've never seen a bad looking feline. Even when they're old and tired, they're exceptional beauties.)

I take Dante's hand in mine. His skin feels real soft. (I don't see fur or feathers though.)

Good sex can be had anywhere, but if it's great sex you're after, *Go thou to Rome.*

The Eternal City has more masterpieces per square foot than any other place in the world. (If you're wondering what's the connection between sex & art, I'll tell you in a moment.) First, let me say this: Rome's small hotels or *pensioni* are the cleanest on the continent. If you can have sex on dirty sheets, bully for you, but in my humble opinion, sex is the cleanest act a man and a woman can ever do together. When you take in oxygen, your blood is purified; when you take in a man you love, your body is refreshed and properly nourished. Clean sheets (especially when you're far away from home) makes for more joyous sex, which is to say, a second orgasm is yours for the asking.

*Go thou to Rome* and you'll discover a conspiracy to keep lovers in-between the sheets. You can't go into a restaurant, or a museum or a church in Rome without being attended to hand and foot. (Good service has a way of increasing the libido, how I don't know, but if you ever had bad service, you know how it can do the opposite.)

*Go thou to Rome* and even the weather is erotic. (Its warm air caresses your skin and before you know it your new-found cheery disposition leads to you-know-what.)

*Go thou to Rome* and you'll discover that its *palazzos,*

*piazzas*, art galleries and Romanesque churches are overcrowded with erotica (every which way you turn male genitalia is what comes up); its beautiful men (some quite alive, thank you) protect you from thinking unhappy thoughts.

It's as if the entire city, prosperous and self-confident, were enclosed in a dome (made-in-Sky-country). If it rains, the transparent dome keeps you dry like an over-sized umbrella. If you're a honeymooner, as Dante and I are, you are protected from the elements, protected from bad fights, protected most of all from bad sex. When you have sex in Rome, you have sex in a protected zone.

Vampires may be born with razor-sharp incisors, but most couples don't get theirs till their wedding night. Then there's no end to things they can do with them in Rome. When they're not hunting each other down, they're off to a *tavola calda*, inspecting its edible art.

*Go thou to Rome* and you'll discover a tangle of cobblestone streets and winding alleys and old courtyards and traffic lights no one notices—even the traffic cops don't obey directions. (In Rome, everyone has the right of way. In Rome, like, everyone's a God in his own right.)

*Go thou to Rome* and you'll have the honour of living forever; you can't see an ancient building intact and not to be convinced you were there when it was erected.

*Go thou to Rome* and you don't have to be a Buddhist to believe in the merits of reincarnation. The capital of the world is overcrowded with angel experts and costumed nuns and little boys and girls urging you to clone them (they're so beautiful).

*Go thou to Rome* and look up the Pantheon, and you will marvel at Roman engineering genius, and exclaim as did Michelangelo: "An angelic and not a human design." (A good travel guide is like a Bible, it quotes the bigwigs.)

*Go thou to Rome* as did Stendhal, Balzac, Wagner, Liszt, Goethe, Gogol, Berlioz, Baudelaire, Keats and Shelley. You may not have a museum as a reward (mind you, Keats and Shelley did), but you may find yourself in the company of Rome's bigwigs ready to quote another bigwig, Henry James, who upon entering the gates of Rome did note: "At last—for the first time—I live!" Or better yet, you can quote Lord Byron: "O Rome! my country! City of the Soul!"

*Go thou to Rome* and quench your thirst. Mind you, while the city boasts over 2,000 water fountains, they're more a feast for your eyes than for your tummy. Wine is the preferred drink of Romans (though supposedly water from the *Fontana di Trevi* near the Spanish Steps makes the best tea).

*Go thou to Rome* but avoid the elegant shops on *Via dei Coronari* which remind you it's good to be rich, and if you're not, sex is a good substitute.

In Florence the *Battistero di San Giovanni*'s "Gates of Paradise" are made of bronze; images of real bigwigs are depicted on their decorative panels—but who cares?

*Go thou to Rome* and any room in any *pensione* with clean sheets and a good lock on its door will make you feel like a bigwig who can catch a glimpse of Eternal Bliss. (Close your eyes and be surprised.)

All roads lead to Rome and now I know why.

In the Vatican you'll find ancient statues of old gods and winged goddesses; you'll find Greek and Etruscan clay pots; you'll find mummified cats and other Egyptian artefacts (you might even find a copy of the Egyptian Book of the Dead if you look hard enough); you'll find Roman military gear and medieval garments worn by church princes; you'll find 16$^{th}$ century tapestries and rare books on alchemy and other forbidden subjects. In the Vatican you'll find what you expect in any good European museum; you'll certainly find a good selection of Renaissance paintings and frescoes; and, of course, if you're lucky and the Sistine Chapel is not closed for repairs (and you weren't stupid enough to wear shorts—can't go in, if you do), you'll find Michelangelo's famous depiction of God, our Father. In the Vatican don't be surprised to hear the words: "No cameras *per piacere*." God (or is it an imposter?) does not want "his" picture taken. Camera-shy.

In the Vatican Dante reminds me of where we met the first time (in Florence, in the *Piazza del Duomo*, in front of the *Battistero di San Giovanni*'s Gates of Paradise); where we had our first cup of coffee (at *La Scogliera*, on *Via Palazzuolo*); where a passerby took a picture of me with his Polaroid on the Medieval stone bridge (*Ponte Vecchio*); and later where we exchanged a quick kiss (in front of a small hat boutique on *Via Roma*) and would have exchanged a lot more had I not been in a hurry to catch a plane.

"I would have looked you up," he tells me, "but I didn't know your name, or where you lived. All I had was the Polaroid shot of you with your phone number—but then I misplaced it, and well, then, I forgot about you. Forgive me?"

I could tell him the truth—I'm not the girl he met years ago in Florence. But I don't.

At the base of the Coliseum where 5,000 wild beasts were slaughtered, and as many early Christians met their end (their martyrdom part and parcel of the local entertainment industry), our tour guide argues television has become the New Coliseum. In the 1950s spectators were satisfied with cowboy and Indian movies, now real shoot-outs are in demand. The Mafia fits the bill.

Dante agrees. In North America Mafia stories have an added bonus. They make Italians look bad, cutting them down to size, and that suits the media moguls just fine. They know the public resents Italians because they have amassed more wealth than any other immigrant group that has ever stepped foot on American soil. How could a bunch of racially inferior, superstitious country hicks from the Southern Italian countryside make the American dream their own (if not for the Mafia?).

"In America everyone can get ahead," says the tour guide. "In Italy if you're born poor, you don't have a chance."

"Unfortunately not everyone gets rich in America," Dante tells him, pointing out that he himself is a third generation Italian-Canadian, and he's presently working as a waiter at his parents' restaurant which might soon go belly-up.

"Oh," says the tour guide and looks me over. Like, if Dante isn't well-to-do, then I am. Suddenly, I'm the one he takes an interest in. Whatever I'm into, he says (wink, wink), he can provide. Cocaine, hashish or heroin?

Dante walks away, and I run after him.

"Don't be angry," I say.

"Why would I be angry?" he asks, angrily. Did he ask

for a big wedding? A honeymoon in Rome? A two bedroom condo in *le Vieux-Montréal*?

Yes, but my mom offered to give them to us. With no strings attached. Should I have said, No?

"Why did you marry me?" he asks. "I have nothing."

Now that I know you, now that I have experienced you like a cloud experiences another cloud: blending, forming, giving birth to strange new art forms, now that we have made love like giant watery creatures do, now that we have combined forces, killed off the Evil One (Loneliness), now that we have seen each other at our best, and better still, at our worst and enjoyed the spectacle, now that our life histories have been re-told, twice, three, four times, now that I am familiar with your likes and dislikes, now that you can read my thoughts and not be frightened, now that you have become my Book of Revelation, now that I have spent time with you viewing sky art, wall art, all kinds of art, seen films, theatre pieces too, now that I have smelled the water of Lourdes in your veins and know it's there, because when I am in pain, it never fails to heal me, now that I have consumed your medicine, now that I know you, I cannot do without you.

Now that I smile when you do, frown when you do, now that you have cleansed me of envy and artifice and hate, now that I have been enveloped in your charms, I can charm anyone (you gave me that power), now that your love is my love, sometimes overwrought with emotion like now—I can't speak, now that I am speechless, I can hear myself moaning, groaning, talking like an animal (in heat), wanting you all over again. Now that my love is feeble because it awaits your love to strengthen it, now that my love longs for your love to prop it up, to give it substance, now that my love crawls towards your love, now that I cannot do without love, now that I am at your feet, a foot soldier wounded in the War of Independence, now that I cannot be independent without you, I ask you to take me, without conditions, with conditions, whatever suits you.

Now that I am at your feet, a supplicant, I plead: let me be your friend, your mate, your cook and secretary, let me feed you with promises, let me feed you with joy, let me feed you, period. Now that you are satisfied, naked and ready for good sex, so am I, and you know it too; how I do love your kiss—smack between my legs ... now that your hands close in on my breasts, nothing is as it should be—it's much better. You dance like an animal in heat, you make love like a semi-divine creature, if you're uninhibited, how can I not be?

Now that you are in my bed, you are my Love Bridge, bridging the gap between have and have not; you are my Venetian vacation, the one I can't afford; now that I am yours I can enjoy imaginary sights, join forces with an army of tourists fighting for a chance to have fun. Now that the future is heavy with possibilities, I seek out your mouth, your arms, your legs, your wings and fly.

Now that my wings are made of invisible fibres: best wishes, my thoughts are electric currents, aiming to please. At the moment conversation does not interest me—what a waste (words!), words have no odour or taste; rather shut up and bring my lips to yours than introduce ideas into the room; I can manage without words, ideas, inventions, but I can't manage without your kiss. Right now I am too far gone, too intoxicated; the smell of your clean body is as potent as a narcotic, it goes up my nostrils and moves me to move unnaturally; right now I am changed from docile awkward plain woman to a beautiful charmer—charming the world for your sake; right now in this room, I smell the presence of God. I know, I said it before, but I have to say it again—God is in your skin, in your touch. I like how you look—your face, your voice and the smell of your skin before you wash and after you scrub off the weariness of having worked yourself to the bone for a good cause: ecstasy (my own).

Now that love has blossomed in your flesh, let me cultivate your good feelings, let me bring you good fortune. I use my tongue to catch raindrops, God's drink, and now I use my tongue to catch yours—holy water; you are my bow & arrow; my toy weapon, my joy.

Now that my tongue is inside your mouth, my tongue seeks to destroy past, present and future—do away with all thought; now that the act is accomplished, I climb into sacred territory. Now that my hands take on your smell, now that what is yours, is mine (no joke), now that your mouth, your tongue, your lungs are mine to share, your will to live is my will to live—and that's it!

I love the baby in you, I love the old man in you, I love you in any shape or form, I think I would love you as pure consciousness, but who cares about that now? Now that your sharp, thorny kisses cut into my skin, this is the end of my life as I know it, thank God!

PART II

# Prayer Books

*Thus spoke Death:*
*I was as you are now, you will be as I am.*

—A TRADITIONAL SAYING

# Chapter 10

This I have heard: Dante is dead. How can this be true?

Nothing has changed. The roads leading into Montréal look no different today than they did yesterday.

Nothing has changed. The sun and the moon rise on cue. Workers do too. Clocks tick. Bells chime. Trains run on time and, if they don't, no one panics.

Nothing has changed. What was, is. The sky is just as beautiful today as it was yesterday, a drawing board fit for the gods to play on.

Nothing has changed. NBC (or is it HBO?) still rules the airwaves. Dante will walk through the door and we'll turn on the TV and watch a good show. In comedy is our salvation (Jesuses abound).

Nothing has changed. The sun, the moon, the stars and my husband's clothes hang where they're supposed to.

Nothing has changed. I can't stop crying—why, I don't know.

Take comfort in your memories, they say, as if memories could be used as a cough tonic, a quick cure. Take comfort in your memories, they say, as if memories could be used as a pillow—lay your head on them, and let your pain go to sleep.

Everything happens for a reason, they say, but they can't give you a reason why a young man's life should be cut short. Time heals all wounds, they say, but it's not true.

Take comfort in your memories, they say, as if memories could help bring back the good times. (They don't!) Take comfort in your memories, they say, as if memories could resurrect the man you love. (They don't!)

The more I think of my dead husband the more it hurts. Remembering offers no solace. Remembering drills a hole in my skull. The memory of my dear husband's I-love-yous (I love you!) enters my brain like a rusted nail. Rather nail me to a cross, then ask me to remember.

It was sunny and now it isn't. Don't give me an umbrella. Take away my sorrow. My husband is dead. How can this be? The day of the car crash, the weather was good; the roads were empty. So how did his car end up in a ditch?

It was sunny and now there are reports of flash floods. Water in my lungs. Water in my brain. Water in my thoughts. Air is a foreign substance. The oxygen racing down my lungs used to have miraculous properties. Not anymore. I can't breathe his air. Eat his food. I'm no thief. What is mine, should be his as well.

The day of the car crash, the weather was good; the roads were empty. His brother, who was in the car with him, did not sustain any injuries. So how is it that my husband's injuries will not heal?

It was sunny and now there are reports of flash floods. Air is a foreign substance. Everything feels foreign, now that he is not here under the umbrella with me.

I find Dante in the kitchen, chopping onions.

"Why did you leave me?" he asks, tears rolling down his cheeks.

And then I wake up.

On my kitchen table: two place settings, two cups, two spoons: sugar for me, honey for him. There's more than enough ...

Some things don't change. Take math. Answers don't change just because someone is in a bad mood or the weather's unfavourable. God shouldn't be able to erase a man's name off the cosmic blackboard as if it were an algebra equation that didn't quite work. Possibly, God is more like a master chef than a mathematician. A chef will keep a favourite recipe on file, but when he doesn't like it anymore—out it goes.

On my kitchen table: food I have no appetite for.

On my kitchen table: reminders I was once loved and now I am not.

My mother finds me dressed in my husband's old clothes.

"You haven't given away his clothes," she says as if to confirm her diagnosis: She's not getting over it.

I would give away my fridge and stove before I would give away his things. The Salvation Army doesn't need them as much as I do. His oversized shirt gives me room to breathe. Like a maternity garment. Like a respirator. An artificial support system.

When I'm down, I put on his sweater (the Golden Fleece!) and wrap its sleeves round my body, and, for a split second, I have the illusion of a hug.

Nothing fits. My loneliness is a fat pig. It eats everything it can, never satisfied.

My apartment is too big. The city is too big.

The hole in the sky is too big. My loneliness, the fat pig, ate it all.

I had wanted a baby in my life as the moon is wanted on a moonless night or the sun is wanted on a cloudy day. I had wanted a baby in my life as eyes are wanted by the sightless or as hearing is wanted by the deaf. I had wanted a baby to come and sit inside my body, use it like a boat and cross from one place to another. Come on board. But no one came. Some babies die at birth. Some die in the womb. And some don't even get a chance to be wished into existence. Not only was the man I loved killed in a car crash, but so was the little baby we would have magically made together. The soul can die many times—before it's born, and afterwards; whenever you lose someone or something you love, it happens.

# Chapter 11

Dragged down to police headquarters and interrogated.

Why was your husband driving your mother's car?

When was the last time the car had been checked?

Did you know the brakes were in poor condition?

Why is your late husband's family refusing to cooperate with the police investigation? (Everyone knows you can't own an Italian restaurant in this city without the Mob's consent.)

Who killed your husband? I'm asked. Was it Mr. Franco Aglieri? A member in good standing of the Queen's Privy Council of Canada and a former treasurer of the Montréal chapter of The Order Sons of Italy.

I recite Psalm 38: *For I will confess my wickedness, and be sorry for my sin …*

Who killed your husband? I'm asked.

"I did it," I tell the police. "I'm responsible for his death. I should have driven his brother to my mother's country house. I knew the roads; my husband did not."

Like that tango (*Malevaje*) says: "*I don't know who I am anymore. I've changed so much. What has God done to me? Yesterday, for fear of killing, instead of fighting, I started running like a hoodlum. I saw myself in jail or dead.*"

Everyone else is getting older; not me though. The pain in my heart feels so fresh, I swear to God, it's like I'm experiencing it for the first time. I'm a real virgin when it comes to being fucked up by grief. One wouldn't think you could be a virgin and a widow; sadly enough, it can be so. Each day that passes by, my husband's death hurts a little more because the reality of it hits me a little more. He isn't late for dinner. He isn't coming home for dinner. Each day I'm getting younger, returning to my youth, my childhood; pain is fresher, betrayal fresher, unhappiness deeper.

There can't be a God. I wasn't sure if there was or wasn't, but now I am. When someone you love dies, then you know there can't be a God. God wouldn't order: "*Thou Shalt Not Kill*" and then do it Himself. There might be a Heaven, but there is no God in it.

Supposedly endorphins kick in at the moment of death and that makes the dying feel good. Too bad endorphins don't kick in when someone you love dies. There are no natural painkillers. Endorphins don't overload your system and make you feel good. Instead, grief kicks in. Grief re-starts your motor—rejuvenating your system and for what? To increase your pain tolerance, why else? When someone you love dies, you didn't think you would be capable of such pain, but you are. That's the beauty of it.

When someone you love dies, you turn into a baby all over again. You see the world with new eyes. A baby's eyes. Like a baby you can look at a hot stove and think you can put your finger on it and it won't hurt. What's a burn mark in comparison to mourning the loss of someone you love?

Grief takes you by surprise. Morning, noon and night. I am always expecting that I'll open the kitchen door and my husband will be there, fixing me supper, helping me out, helping me remember I'm no baby—I can get over this. But he's never there.

I wish I were a baby, then I could grow up. But I'm baby-less—or shell-less. I have been stripped of my protective covering and now anyone or anything can prey on me.

*Thou shalt not kill.* Only a Baby would think it could get away with murder.

On the kitchen table: freshly-caught brook trout.

Dante cuts one open and asks: "Why did you leave me?"

And then I wake up.

"You had a bad dream," says Guido.

"Don't make anything of it," says Guido.

"Don't cry," says Guido.

"Give it time," says Guido.

I yell at him: "You expect me to go back to work as if nothing had happened. But something did happen."

"You don't have to go back to work," he says. "When my grandfather died I stayed at home for a while. I couldn't function. I couldn't bear the idea I wouldn't see him again. Growing up I had shared my room with him. In Italy he had made his living as a musician, he played the accordion at weddings, and sang at funerals. But here he found it hard to find work. People didn't trust him and all because he shared the same name as Montreal's notorious Mafia crime boss, Vic Cotroni. Actually, kids at school often teased me about my name. They assumed my father was a hit man. My grandfather was the one who taught me how to stand up to bullies. He said violence begets violence, calm begets calm. To survive in the jungle animals use camouflage; humans can do likewise. He advised me to blend in; to become a mirror image of those in power. If I managed to get it right, I would be left alone, and then I would be free to do whatever I wished. I did what he said, and in no time, I became indistinguishable from my classmates and I thrived. My grandfather saved my hide. I owe my success to him. When I opened my dental office, I made sure that I addressed my clients in the language of their choice—English, Italian, Parisian French, French *joual* or *Franglais*. My landlord, Franco Aglieri, does likewise. In fact, as soon as the *Office québécois de la langue française* indicated that the English neon sign on his office tower, *Complex Aglieri*, broke the law, he had it torn down and replaced with the appropriate French equivalent. His reward—the Mayor's chief party fundraiser rents an entire floor at *Complexe Aglieri*. My grandfather was my mentor and my hero. He understood the ways of the world. I miss him."

"Why are you telling me all this, Guido?"

"You never have to work another day in your life. I will take care of you, Sophie. Move in with me."

"And why would I do that?" I ask, kicking him. Shouting obscenities. But it's not Guido I want to pick a fight with. It's Dante I want to hurt. When he was still alive, we never argued. We hadn't known each other long enough, I guess. I never even saw him wake up on the wrong side of the bed. If I had, it might be easier now to forget his divine good looks, his good-natured temperament and his ridiculous need to love me.

I try to imagine what Dante would have looked like as an old man, but I can't.

I ask Guido: "Where were you the night my husband was killed?"

"Am I a suspect?"

"Everyone is."

Nothing fits. Even my shoes don't fit right. I put on Dante's moccasins and turn on the computer, wishing I could email him. Native Americans used to believe the living could contact the dead. All you had to do was walk into a forest, say a few chants and, before you knew it, you had access to your ancestors who, if they chose, could help you out.

Isn't it odd the more civilized we become, the more we imitate our animal cousins? E.g., a baby elephant dies, his mother grieves—but only for a short period (about four days). That's what's expected of us too—if someone you love dies, Come on, get over it. There must be a correlation between the use of high tech and the return to our animal heritage. Animals eat on the run, animals live common-law (no marriage ties, thank you), animals don't bother with rites of passage, no churches, no grieving either. Grieving is an archaic pastime, reserved for superstitious folk. Who needs medicine men or voodoo priestesses? We don't need their false knowledge of God. We have high tech now: iPhones, iPads, instant messaging, Dr. Google, smart homes, smart cars, space shuttles racing to Mars and beyond —living proof we're a cut above simple machines. And animals. And gods too.

You can have whatever you like in life, but grief is something else. Grief is something you're not allowed to have. Another banned substance.

When I turn on my laptop, it reminds me of who I am not. I can't gain entry into Dante's email account. I don't know his password. I never asked him. If I had, I might now know who had him killed. And why.

It is easier to swim across the *Saint-Laurent* river than it is to find a soul mate. I found mine, and now he is dead.

Native Americans used to make little holes in the shoes of their newborns in the belief that, if the gods saw that their newborns didn't have a good pair of shoes, then they couldn't make the long journey to the Land of the Dead. They had to live!

I take off Dante's moccasins and put on my running shoes, wishing I could be allowed to enter the Land of the Dead and look for Dante.

"And then, Sophie, my soul left my body and I was on the ceiling looking down on my body, unconcerned. And then my travel guide—(Sophie, don't worry, everyone gets one)—took me to the Great Pyramid at Giza. The place covers thirteen acres and contains more than two million blocks of stone. It's one of the wonders of the world and if it isn't, Sophie, it should be. Oh Sophie, I wish you had come with me. Why did you leave me?"

And then I wake up.

When a Scythian king died (ca. 9th century BC) his belly was slit open, cleaned out, and filled with various aromatic substances like parsley seeds and anise. Then the slit was sewn up and the body coated over with wax.

When an ancient Roman died, coins were placed on his eyelids—as an advance for the ferryman in Hades who would carry the deceased across the river to his new home.

Nowadays when a monk dies in Tibet, his body is cut up and fed to the birds.

When a Canadian dies, his widow or widower is responsible for the funeral costs. The Aglieris hand me the bill. It's more than I make in a year.

I argue—I didn't order the solid oak coffin with brass handles ...

Yes, but as I refused to believe Dante was dead, they had to make the funeral arrangements ...

"Who identified the body?" I ask, suddenly wondering if there actually was a body. What if the accident was part of an elaborate cover-up? What if Dante is in a witness protection program, with a new identity? What if Dante told the police everything he knew—his uncle is using his parents' restaurant to launder the proceeds of criminal activities? What if Dante is alive and well and I'm just a shadow of my former self? A pariah. Penniless and cursed.

# Chapter 12

The circus is back in town. Sandra Wolfe, the ring master, says: Come on in, the show's almost ready to roll. The audience—delegates from the Tall Towers' Club—are in on the act. Call it interactive entertainment for high society.

Feel like a midget. Actually, I always feel like a midget next to my mother. She is half a foot taller than I am. When I'm with her, I can enter any room and go unnoticed. Mother's famous and that should be a cause for celebration. Why then, every time she is recognized on the street, in a restaurant, do I want to hide? I can't bear it. It's like standing next to a tourist attraction. Everyone wants to take a picture of you. Actually, one time a woman asked me to get out of the way so she could focus on my mother, and then someone told her that I was *Sandra Wolfe*'s daughter, and suddenly she was all apologetic. Basically she was telling me I had no intrinsic value of my own, only as *Sandra Wolfe*'s daughter did I have worth.

The problem isn't that my mother is an egomaniac, a

veritable monster. She isn't. (She is quite nice actually.) My mother is more like a friendly giant. It is easier to deal with a monster. A monster is out to kill you; you know what you're up against. But a friendly giant rolls over you, and it's an accident. She doesn't mean to kill you; she is just big because she is big. She can't help herself.

To survive, to retain a sense of integrity, I became the opposite of what my mother is. She hogs the limelight; I shy away from it. I like being ordinary. I like not having to prove anything. I like being anonymous. Going unnoticed. I don't want to be a freak; anyone who is famous is a freak. Possibly God himself is the Ultimate Freak, but that's another story. God can't be on Mom's show though. God is too busy building another universe—one in which life and death are interchangeable. If wood can burn, turn to ash, why shouldn't ash just as easily be turned back into wood? If Hollywood can make it happen in the movies, why shouldn't God be able to do it?

I doubt the giants my mother is interviewing on her show care whether or not there is life after death—they're well-adjusted and well-to-do. In the business world the taller a person tends to be, the more successful he is. The little guy has to pack a gun to inspire fear; all a giant has to do is breathe.

The expert interviewed on the show corroborates what we all suspect: the taller you are, the more money you make. Each inch on your frame represents X number of dollars. Members of tall clubs can lord over the rest of us and get away with it. The men are seen as action heroes, and the ladies, models, venerated for their statuesque good looks, long legs and flawless bikini areas.

"Not so fast," argues one of the delegates, wearing a T-shirt with the words: "I may be the first to be rained on, but I won't be the first to be drowned." The world caters to people of average height. It's not much fun trying to fit into their clothes or walk through their doorways. And being thought of as a basketball player because of your height (when you don't give a damn about any kind of sport) is real bothersome.

Soon the pros and cons of being tall are debated on live TV. This is as much a circus of ideas, as of images. In medieval times you didn't have to be an intellectual to host a freak show exhibiting "human oddities." Zookeepers would do. But nowadays, the more grey matter tucked in your skull, the better chances you have of keeping your act together and showing off "The World's Greatest Freaks, Past and Present."

After the show, off camera, the host admits to everything: violence is pornographic, but not as much as one's innermost secrets. Erudition, wit and personality are valued in a television talk show host, but unless he can use it to get a star to confess his sins, he should get out of the business. Lining freaks and verbally shooting them down can get you good ratings or bad ones (depending on the mood of the nation). One week she's told to be aggressive, hostile even, and the next, she's advised to be holier than thou, a Larry King clone. Stand-up comics have taken over late-night talk shows. Soon they'll fill in all the daytime slots too—and then she might have to stand on her head or wear a gas mask. Competition is stiff. Producers want the host to entertain, enlighten—and at the same time, stick to inanities. Like what do drag queens wear to bed? And do they pee standing up or sitting down? Do daredevils have safe sex or do they get their jollies putting their lives on the line? Talk show hosts are supposed to make the audience laugh. Who goes to a circus to laugh? Okay, everyone loves a clown, but they're thrown in for comic relief. It's the big acts—flying Dumbos—who steal the show. That's why her show's so popular. Each one of her guests runs the risk of making a fool of himself.

Tabloid television goes in for the kill—why be hypocritical about it? What was her highest rated show? Guess? Did it deal with (take your pick): breast implants, the death penalty, abortion, gay rights, transvestite beauty pageants, angel sightings, UFO sightings, men who get their jollies being spanked, men who get their jollies wearing diapers ... Close. Her highest rated show featured naked people. They sat with newspapers over their laps—you couldn't see a thing, but enough to know the guys & dolls weren't wearing undies. That show was a step up from last year's varied offerings. (Sandra Wolfe, the Freak Keeper, really went out on a limb!) Victims (any which kind) were all the rage then.

Listen, moral gatekeepers of America, talk show hosts are not. On the quest for higher ratings, anything goes. Voyeurism is in, let the good times roll ...

All true ... But ma, the reason I'm here is because, well, ma ...

"I need money," I tell her. "I'm expected to pay for Dante's funeral expenses. His parents got a private loan from you know who, and now they're expected to pay it back, with interest. If they don't, who knows what will happen?"

"Poor baby," she says. "Would 5 grand be enough?"

"No."

"Then there is a problem," she says. Her funds are tied up. She can't liquidate them at a moment's notice.

I accuse her of not loving him.

"Not true," she says. She'd love anyone I loved.

"Precisely—you didn't take the time to know him!"

"No matter what I do, it's never enough," she says.

I'm a bad girl—I admit it. I'm ungrateful. I almost feel as if it were some outside (evil!) force that is making it impossible for me to love my mother.

My mother doesn't notice I'm drunk or if she does, she doesn't say anything. Soon I might turn into a real drunk, roaming around like a tormented shadow, drinking because of anger, because of grief, because I don't belong anywhere. I see myself anywhere but at home. A home I can no longer afford. A home which is no longer mine. Dante's things are in it. It's his place, not mine.

My mother tells me: "Dante left you his share of the restaurant, *Chez Nina*. It's in a good location. When the insurance money comes through, you'll have more than enough. You'll be fine."

"The police suspect arson," I remind her.

"Dante's family can air their complaints on my show. Talk to them." Hinting, hinting, hinting. If I can get Dante's parents to go on her show and talk about what it is like being related to Montreal's Mob boss, she would make it worth my while.

If I did, would I be making a pact with the Devil? I can't think of my very own mom as a horned creature. I can't think at all. Right now my head is hurting. I am totally drunk or not drunk at all. It's not like me to drink. I just wanted to get rid of the metallic taste in my mouth, wash off the taste of grief.

Oh mommy, I tell her, don't involve yourself in Dante's family affairs. It was bad enough my husband was killed because he knew too much. Does she want to be next in line?

"Don't be paranoid," she says. "The Mob has no interest in me."

She takes out her cheque book, and says: "Tell me how much you need."

I don't answer.

Here I am a supplicant, re-establishing dependency on the friendly giant. I've proven her right—I can't make it on my own. I am dependent on her, and I resent her because I resent my dependency. She's a tree and I'm a little twig—that's just how it is. Everything I own is hers. Even my body is hers more than mine. (She made me, didn't she?)

I tell her: "If I hadn't been financially dependent on you, if I had had my own car, instead of your old one, Dante would be alive."

"Stop blaming yourself," she says, handing me a cheque.

I look at it, and all I feel is anger. Anger because I can make do without a husband's love, but I can't make do without cash. Flashes of self-deprecation and self-pity surface, but no self-love. Self-love went out the window when Dante flew off into the unknown—unaccompanied, a victim of a hit-and-run. I should have been the one killed. I should have been in the driver's seat. It was my car, not his. He's dead because of me.

I take my mother's cheque and tear it in half.

Here she is trying to do the right thing (pay my debts), she's coming through, doing the best she can, and I accuse her. I am so mean. So harsh on her. Why? Why can't I get used to her celebrity? No one else minds it, but me.

"You're not my mother," I tell her. "I was adopted. Why, I was, I don't know. All I know is that you can't be my mother. You're tall and I'm short. You're smart and I'm not."

My mother (my adopted mother) turns white as a ghost.

Everything is blurry. On the coffee table: a copy of John Milton's *Paradise Lost*. The author was blind. And me? Everything is blurry. I am looking for something, but I don't remember what it is I am looking for. Everything is blurry. Is the Otherworld a real place or an imaginary one? If it's real, why do we have to die to get there? Everything is blurry. I don't even know why I am on all fours, looking under the table. Is it a book I lost? Or a key?

"You were looking for your husband's old photos," a voice in my head tells me.

"*Late* husband," I correct.

And then I realize I'm *late* for an appointment. How can the word "*late*" mean two different things? It must be a sign of collective dementia. Memory loss *par excellence*. That's why the world is in such a mess. No one remembers anything. Everything is blurry.

I walk into the bedroom and there's Dante looking through the drawers. He's dressed as he often was—in jeans and a T-shirt.

"I thought you were dead," I tell him, about to embrace him.

"There's no time for that now," he says. "You wanted to know where my old photos were, well, I've come to tell you that they're here, in the bottom drawer."

I look where he says, and there are the old pictures: Dante's first steps ... First Holy Communion ... first trip to Italy ... And here's the girl he met in Florence. She looks just like me: same hair, same skin, the same look of bewilderment.

"Why did you leave me?" he asks.

And then I wake up.

Back at work, I turn on the lights of the antique shop and immediately know something is amiss. I check behind the antique dressers, pull out the drawers of an old secretary desk, unlock the doors of a rosewood bookcase—nothing. I expect a haunting spirit to announce its arrival; expect a sensation of cold or heat but I don't expect what I get—Guido on the floor, on all fours, looking up at me—unshaven and unwashed.

"How did you get in?" I ask.

"The back door was open," he answers. Why he came through the back door, he doesn't say. Why he's carrying a sack over his shoulder, he doesn't say either.

I offer him tea in an antique set, explaining the reason why the cups are so small is because back in the 18$^{th}$ century tea cost as much as coke—cocaine, that is.

Guido is not interested in antiques. What he wants to tell me is that his grandfather's burial service will take place on the Venetian mainland. Wagner and Ezra Pound were buried there, and now his grandfather will share the soil with them. Ever since he was a boy, he tells me, he accompanied his grandfather to Venice in the summer and took in its *palazzi* and old churches and covered bridges and outdoor cafes. If God were to ask him to give him proof that people are superior to animals, would he dish out the latest iPhone or GPS device? Oh no. He would give God a tour of Venice.

"Don't fool yourself," I say. "You don't love Venice because your grandfather was born there. You love it because that's where you met your wife."

"I doubt it," he says, opening the sack he came in with. In it—his grandfather's accordion.

Guido puts the accordion on his lap; opens it gently, as if it were a swaddled child, in need of changing. Guido starts to play the accordion (I didn't even know he could play) and out comes a tango.

"Dante was a tango instructor, but you knew that—didn't you?" I ask.

"Why wouldn't I have known it? The tango was his weapon of choice."

"The wrong choice."

And then, he plays the *Abandono,* humming the lyrics: "*Now I don't dream that you will return to the failure of my life. I only wish that if you are also on the cross of abandonment you'll know how to forgive me in your mercy. The past accuses me. I don't know if you will live happily, or if the world has defeated you, if living without wanting to live, you seek the peace of dying. I hear voices that name you again and again. You are good.*"

I wonder: can an instrument have a soul? One expects cats and dogs to live after they die, but do instruments find their way to the Otherworld? The squeeze box is not popular anymore (been replaced by the guitar)—but who is to say it's not popular in Heaven? Lots of old-timers there. An accordion is a weapon against low spirits, I decide. It's possible angels like the sound of the instrument. I can't imagine they would limit themselves to harps ... It is assumed angels use their wings to fly, but what if the creatures don't need wings to propel themselves through space? What if their wings are musical instruments? We play the accordion with our fingers. What if an angel can play his accordion-pleated wings with his thoughts? Open them up and have music any time of the day?

At the end of the tune, Guido hands me his grandfather's accordion and says: "I want you to have it."

"I can't take it," I say. "It has been in your family for generations. Give it to your children."

"*L'amore comincia co lo suono e canto, e va finire con un mare di pianto,*" he says, replacing the accordion in the sack.

"With song and music love will start, but in a sea of weeping part," I reply translating the Italian proverb.

Had I swum across the English Channel, I would have shocked him less.

"Since when do you speak Italian?" he asks.

"Ever since I can remember."

"Did Dante know you speak Italian?"

"Of course," I say, lying.

I expect reprimands—Liar, liar, pants on fire! I expect accusations, put-downs, a shouting match, anything but what I am treated to: sobs.

"Did you ever love me?" he asks.

"Too much," I tell him, but he doesn't believe me.

# Chapter 13

*Time Magazine* reports that, if the universe collapses back on itself in The Big Crunch, it may tunnel through a wormhole to create a new universe. *Time Magazine* reports that the universe may have been born out of the collapse of another universe fifteen billion years ago, which tunnelled through hyperspace to create The Big Bang. It's possible, *Time Magazine* reports, that neighbouring universes exist alongside our own.

*Time Magazine* does not report that God is the ultimate Handyman, ready to fix up the universe at a moment's notice. *Nor* does it report that a universe is easier to fix than a widow's grief. If it were easier, Mr. Fix-It would do it, but He can't.

The downtown Hilton is teeming with out-of-towners: Klingons, Romulans, Ferengi and Captain Kirks, buying and selling; partying. This communication officer can't get her act together.

Am I at a *Star Trek* convention or at a lecture on quantum physics?

An aeronautical engineer-scientist from Stanford University tells us that one day soon a spaceship will be able to travel thousands of miles per second using hydrogen gas sucked up from space itself. If the spaceship flew through a wormhole, it could cross galactic distances instantly. You could get a tour of a distant planet, star or galaxy in no time. (No joke.)

The Stanford fellow is also convinced that one day soon you will be able to fax yourself to another part of the universe—everything in your body (cells, tissue, thoughts, memories) can be converted into computer code and then transmitted anywhere you like. (No joke.)

And where is God in all this? Is the Sweet (Wo)Man working round the clock—trying to undo his mistakes? Things wear out. (Cosmic Law.) The universe will wear out too. It could be God has become attached to his little creation, he doesn't want to start another from scratch. (He has the recipe, so it's no big deal.) It could be God delegated control of our solar system to his angels. (Offspring? Clones? Or what?) Could be angels are keeping tabs on us. Are we a race of misogynists or philanthropists?

Can't concentrate ... Turn to page 69 in your *Star Trek* manual. What language is the lecture in anyway?

"Blejeghebe chugh voj blhegh."

Klingon.

What language do the dead speak in? Binary code? One can buy a dictionary for Klingon at a local bookstore, but one assumes one's ancestors speak one's language—no dictionary required.

Does my late husband speak Italian or English to his

great grandparents? Linguists tell us thought precedes language; a telepath wouldn't need a dictionary or a translator; instant communication.

Stop.

*Arrête.*

I can't concentrate. I lost my place on the page. I lost my place in history. When I lost my husband, I lost touch with God. The loss was that big. When I lost my husband, I lost my way.

Where is Captain James Tiberius Kirk? I want to ask the captain of the Starship Enterprise if the Otherworld is in outer space or inner space.

Someone asks: True or false: first interracial kiss happened on *Star Trek*?

Someone answers: Beam me up, Scotty ...

The guest lecturer doesn't say anything about the underlying principle of the cosmos: *something is better than nothing*. I'm the one who lets the crowd in on the secret.

All eyes turn to me. Let them look. Death is kicking my face in. And theirs too. What am I doing at a *Star Trek* Convention? I was never a diehard fan. Dante was though.

Dante is not here. I keep looking for him, hoping to find him here. Like that tango (*Que Falta Que Me Haces*) says: "*How I long to find him, after so many nights of being alone, without him, how I long to embrace him. How much I need him. How long are the hours now that he is not here. If only I could find him, if only he could see the tenderness I have to give to him, it would be enough to make the world his.*"

The Vulcan sitting next to me is no substitute for the man I lost, but I don't care. I don't care about anything anymore. Dante is not here.

A stranger is in my husband's bed.

Liquor robs you of common sense. Liquor robs you of moral fortitude. Liquor robs you of fear. If you get robbed when you're drunk, too bad. Drunk, you deserve to be taken for what you're worth.

"What are you talking about? You didn't drink a thing," Dr. Lee assures me.

I don't remember inviting him to sleep over. I hadn't even allowed Guido to enter my bedroom, and now here is this stranger, prancing around naked. I don't even know his first name. Someone is called Doctor and suddenly it doesn't matter what his name is. And whether he is married or not. If a man can heal your body, he can heal your spirit.

Dr. Lee's a compulsive talker, yap, yap; like a flustered girl, he can't wait to tell me his secrets. He doesn't understand I don't want to know his secrets. I don't want him in my life.

I allowed this man to sleep on my husband's pillow. How could I have?

I can't forgive myself for doing it. Forgiveness is too quick a fix.

Biochemists tell us an infant finds its mother's nipple through smell, and a mother can pick out her newborn based on its scent alone. Smell is essential to communication. Humans can discern 10,000 or more odours. Each of us has his own smell or odour-print as unique as the whorls on our fingers. It can't be scrubbed off—it's ours for keeps.

I caught a glimpse of my late husband each time I smelled his pillow. Saw him leaning towards me, a nice smile on his lips. And now another man slept on his pillow! Another thing to throw out ...

The Talking Head can't shut himself up. He says most

doctors (not him though) insist the near-death experience (NDE) and its accompanying high are a result of any one or more of the following:

- *oxygen deprivation;*
- *metabolic changes due to a sudden release of hormones, endorphins (overwhelming one with feelings of joy, beauty, love and peace);*
- *drugs given to reduce pain (LSD, peyote and other psychedelic drugs can simulate an NDE);*
- *wish fulfilment (one's brain wants to live forever and so it convinces one that it can);*
- *or if one takes the Freudian position, an NDE is one's memory of being born—one goes down a dark vaginal tunnel and out into the light.*

The Talking Head says he doesn't buy into any of the above theories. He had a Near-Death-Experience and now he has no fear of death. His own NDE (as a result of a diving accident) convinced him the Otherworld is more beautiful than this one. He saw angels without wings, libraries without ceilings (the stacks went on and on), and books without covers—with one look you understood everything in them.

The Talking Head says he is involved in paranormal research.

Now I remember how he seduced me. Or why I had seduced him. I had bartered sex for inclusion in his study!

The medical research centre is a veritable maze. In Room 101A: obligatory rats.

In Room 104B: pickled ears, eyes, and tongues. In Room 112C: out-of-body experiments (OBEs) are under investigation. The researchers aim to duplicate an OBE in a controlled laboratory setting. No study has ever proved the existence of an astral body or spirit double which could leave its host and travel on its own. Tangible proof could lead to a Nobel Prize.

Dr. Lee's assistant preps me for the experiment. Clamps electrodes on my head and activates the right temporal lobe ...

Can my spirit double pop out of my body and read the numbers written on the ceiling?

Dr. Lee is unsure of his rights. Can he stay the night, or call it a night? He reminds me of Dante—never mind, he's Chinese. It's not his looks which remind me of him. It's his insistence that I'm a beautiful woman. Give a man a blow job, and suddenly he's visually impaired. The man smells too clean—like Javel. He's too young, too pleasant, too easy to please. And full of hot air.

The Talking Head says the state of consciousness can be altered. All you need is the belief that you can't be limited by the physical world; the laws of space and time don't apply to your soul or essence.

OBEs can be self-induced, he insists. And you don't need drugs or state-of-the-art equipment. LSD, peyote and other psychedelic drugs can produce out-of-body experiences, but it's best to do it on your own. Call it a form of self-hypnosis. Just don't call it self-delusion.

The Talking Head says he pops out of his body all the

time (*sans* drugs). I hadn't been able to do it at the lab—but not to worry. I'll get it right the next time.

I turn the corner and there's the most beautiful garden I have ever seen.

The flowers come in many shapes and colours; some of them have geometrical patterns. A luminous being is watering the plants. (Actually, he's not really watering them; what pours out of the hose is a luminous ethereal substance.)

The gardener stops me and says: "He that enters Paradise must have the Golden Key."

I look in my purse; all I find are my car keys.

The flowers lock stems and throw off a bad stench.

And then the phone rings.

"Why did you leave me?" asks Dante.

And then I wake up.

# Chapter 14

A talk show host is like a medium—he is establishing communication with individuals he'll never meet in the flesh. Vacuum land is one big spirit world.

Con artists make the best mediums. Don't know about talk show hosts (research pending).

Do know Nielsen ratings spook talk show hosts. If the numbers go up, it proves somebody is actually out there; when the ratings go down, it just goes to show you nothing lasts forever.

Bring in the clowns ...

Seasoned Talk Show Host, Sandra Wolfe, introduces her first guest—St. Joan of Arc, actually, *Jeanne d'Arc.* Actually, her channeller ... "I saw angels with my bodily eyes as clearly as I see you. And when they departed, I wept and wished that they had taken me with them."

"Joan-ny, hold that thought." Commercial break ...

Talk show guest, St. Joan of Arc, is followed by an ESP demonstration, followed by a man who claims he can bend metal objects with his mind and proves it too by twisting a silver spoon. PK or psychokinetic powers have nothing to do with the spirit world, he says, science can explain it: there are different kinds of brain waves—beta, alpha, theta and delta. The speed of their emissions differs. Meditation, listening to music and so on can affect emissions. Control them and you control the physical world. Anyone can do it.

Guest no. 4 is less modest. Faith healing is a gift of the Holy Ghost, and few are lucky enough to be given it. (That's why he asks for donations.) Guest no. 5 disagrees—she's a Catholic nun and a massage therapist. She believes the Holy Ghost will help those who help themselves. The healing properties of touch have long been exploited in the East, and there's no reason Western medicine shouldn't incorporate it.

The best is saved for the last: an internationally acclaimed medium ...

Medium (to a member of the audience): "I see the spirit of a man with dark eyes who wants to talk to you."

Audience member: "It must be my husband."

Medium: "He says he loves you."

Audience member: "Ask him—is there life after death?"

Medium: "He says, there is no death!"

Audience member: "Where is he now?"

Medium: "Summer Land."

Audience Member: "Heaven?"

Medium: "Summer Land."

Audience member: "Ask him—is there a hell?"

Medium: "People are good by nature; there is no need for hell."

Big applause.

The dialogue sounds familiar. I bet it was copied from a book. (I may have read it!) In the late 19th century, when spiritualism was at its height (President Abraham Lincoln and his wife, Mary, regularly hosted séances at the White House) the then popular mediums, the Fox sisters, often spoke of Summer Land. It wouldn't surprise me if the so-called member of the audience was actually an actress who rehearsed the scene with the current internationally acclaimed medium prior to the show. Anything goes.

Back to business. Back to the treachery of life. Real life.

There—on the conference table—lies the picture of my double. Proof I was adopted, proof I have a twin.

The woman who calls herself my mother examines the picture. (Demands a magnifying glass.)

"There's an uncanny resemblance," she admits, "but Sophie, she isn't your twin. I had one daughter and it's you."

Her staff examine the picture and admit the girl and I look alike. I betcha one of my mother's Italian housemaids had twins out of wedlock. My mother, feeling sorry for her (or for herself!), offered to take one of the infants off her hands, and here I am. If I were adopted, it would explain why I don't look like my mother, I don't sound like her and I certainly don't smile all the time like she does. I am too lonely to smile. I'm always looking for a sister.

"We should find out who the girl in the photo is," my mother says. "There's a phone number on the back."

"It doesn't work," I say.

And then I see that look in her eyes. I know it straight off—she has an idea for a new show.

Like a spider she extends her web to catch whatever she can for her supper. It doesn't matter the victim has to be killed first. Spiders are merciful—anaesthetize their victims first. Not Sandra Wolfe. If it makes for a good story, you do what you got to do.

"If we did a show on doubles," she says, knowing I found her out, "we could put all our resources into motion."

The look on my face must be transparent, because the next thing that comes out of her mouth is: "You never accepted me, Sophie. You would have liked anyone else but me to be your mother. First it was your nanny; you adored her. She only spoke Italian, and that made her even more endearing to you. I begged her to come to Canada with us. She refused. Employees are like that—they'll love you as long as it's convenient. And then there was our next door neighbour, Carmela. You idolized her. She made spaghetti, you loved it. I did it, it was no good."

"You never cooked," I say. "You were too busy being famous."

"It's ironic," she says. "You resent me because I have a career and I resented my mother because she didn't have one. Had she been happy, I would have forgiven her for her lack of drive, but she was in tears all the time. She had one miscarriage after another, and it destroyed her. She had imagined herself having a brood of youngsters to tend to and adore, but all she had was me. And I wasn't nearly enough. She was anxious all the time. She stuck around me like a bodyguard, afraid I would disappear if she didn't constantly watch over me. I couldn't wait to leave that house. My mother was inadvertently killing my spirit. I managed to get a scholarship to Yale and I made my escape. And then when I least expected it, a year before you were born, she died and I was lost. I longed for her protection. Her presence. I wore her ring but it did not comfort me. That year I replaced my father's family name with hers. That helped me cope with the loss. Every time someone calls me, *Madame* Wolfe, I think of my mother, and I have the illusion she is in the room. I'm safe."

She returns the picture to me. "It's okay, sweetheart. We don't have to do a show on doubles."

Always so damn fair.

"We can do a series on antiques," she says. "The timing is right. You could be a consultant." Like, no strings attached.

"Go ahead, do a show on doubles," I say. "Find out who the woman in the picture is."

Even if the girl in the picture isn't a blood relative, she's one in spirit. If she hadn't noticed Dante in Florence noticing her, Dante might not have noticed me, noticing him and then I would never have understood it should be better to have loved and lost than not to have loved at all; alas, it ain't so.

# Chapter 15

Death is an undiscovered country until someone you love enters it, and then, the mystery is all gone. He's discovering it for you, sending you pictures, spirit postcards from the other side. Except the mail is stalled. If my late husband had gone off to live in a space station, I could have a conversation via satellite with him; if he had gone off to war, I could probably get word to him. So why is it that, now he's dead, I can't contact him?

At the turn of the last century wives of Italian men who went off to work in North America were called white widows. Their husbands could just as well have been dead, living as far away as they did. Every one of them promised to return home, but not all did. Once you immigrate, you're free of the past.

Guido begs to differ.

"In Italy Northerners blame Southerners for their problems and Southerners blame Northerners," he says. "But once they cross the Atlantic, old divisions go out the window. It doesn't matter if the newcomers toss their pasta in red sauce (Southern style) or in cream (Northern style), everyone is a Wop. Everyone is treated like a second-class citizen. Everyone is discriminated against."

"I should have heeded your advice, Guido. The Algieris are not to be trusted."

"Italians don't go around killing each other," he says. "The Mob wasn't involved in your husband's death. It was an accident."

"Dante's uncle is in jail," I remind him.

"The man was framed."

"But, Guido, it was you who told me the Algieris spelled trouble. I had to avoid them."

"I would have done and said anything to win you back."

"All is fair in love and war?"

"Sophie, Franco Algieri, is not in the Mafia. And even if he were, in Montréal, crime bosses don't support old-style gangster strategies. They opt for legitimate business practices; they recognize the authority of the state. They don't target rival families. Big businesses prefer cartels to hit men ... Can you believe it? The police have knocked on my door and asked me questions—Why is Franco Aglieri my landlord? My client? In this city dentists are a dime a dozen, but, if an Italian has a good practice, then he's in with the Mob."

"You're always complaining," I say.

"Italians invented the language of complaint. They figured it out long before anyone else that it's easier to move from one country to another (easier to start over) than it is to be happy. It's easier to move out of the lower classes—

go from being the son of a house painter, to being a dentist with a good practice—than it is to be happy."

"You sound like my late husband," I say.

His expression, his accent, his self-pity also remind me of him.

I look at his hands and they too remind me of Dante's. And then I know I must never see him again.

It's Christmas and Santa Clauses are patrolling *rue Sainte-Catherine*. Dressed to kill, I look for someone to un-love, un-know, un-discover. I seek someone to strip me of my thoughts or my clothes. Don't care which comes first.

I want someone to take over my body, because I don't want the job anymore. If I could undress myself of my flesh, if I could unburden myself of this world's falsehoods: false gold, false hope, false friends (even our blue skies lack substance) and be sure to meet the man I love, I would do it. But you can't commit suicide and expect a welcoming committee. You can't enter the Otherworld, unless you're invited first.

A trip around this world might do me good, but I can't afford it. Cruising the downtown bars doesn't cost me a penny. Travellers from all over the world come and park their bodies at the Ritz-Carlton Hotel. If you're looking to meet an angel, there's no better place.

The bartender agrees. Like an actor he's trained to ignore your boos/boo-ze. If you pay someone to serve you, you pay someone to like you. (It's included in the price.) A good tip absolves you of any wrongdoing. Charity on-the-go.

Put a toonie inside a vending machine, and out comes

a Coke; put one in a jukebox and out comes a tango (*De Puro Curda*): "*Hey waiter, give me another vodka. I don't care what people say. I don't want to be decent. I don't want to be human. It hurts too much.*" Put out a smile in a bar and the 300-pound man next to you is yours for the asking.

I smile and the man next to me at the bar says he has a guardian angel. It's his cat. Do I want to meet him?

A sucker for angel-cats, I follow the man to his room.

It doesn't matter if there's an angel-cat or not, I'm too lonesome to care ...

Do you want the lights on or off? I'm asked.

Yes, to another blackout.

Yes, to another kiss.

Yes, to another man whom I pity.

He frees himself of his desire and I free myself of guilt. I should have been driving Dante to my mother's house. I should have been in the driver's seat. I should have died in the car accident. Not my husband.

The fat cat has no comment. (Fast asleep.)

The bad girl tiptoes out of the room, taking the man's prized possession: the angel-cat, of course. You don't have to be a friendly giant to be in need of one.

My room is a mess. My thoughts are a mess.

On the news: the body of a man was found in the trunk of a car in *Saint-Léonard*, Québec. The police suspect Mafia involvement.

On the news: Italy's top court convicts two top Mafia bosses of having plotted the bombing in Palermo that killed a top anti-Mafia prosecutor.

I can't sleep. I can't leave the house. Am too spooked. I can't return the angel-cat to its rightful owner. He has left town, and so should I.

On the news: floods, earthquakes. Lock your doors—a serial rapist is on the loose.

On the news: record cold temperatures. The wind is howling. Not half as loud as the voices in my head. Watch out, Sophie Wolfe, the Mafia will do you in.

Legend has it everyone has two angels: an angel of justice, and an angel of evil. The angel of justice is tender, reserved, sweet and peaceful. The angel of evil, on the other hand, is quick to anger, full of bitterness and madness. You know him by his work.

Who killed my husband? Was it an angel of evil or an angel of justice who pointed to Dante Aglieri and decided let's get rid of Sophie Wolfe's love interest? She needs to be taught a lesson. She needs to suffer.

Legend has it that X number of years ago the Devil tried to wrestle control of the universe from The Rightful Heir. One third of God's angel army sided with the Devil, the rest stayed on with the Commander-in-Chief.

Legend has it that, when the celestial war ended, the borders between Heaven and Hell were drawn for all eternity. The Earth is another matter. It became a surrogate battlefield; humans, war trophies for God and the Devil.

Legend has it that God is the Good Guy, and the Devil, the Nazi sympathizer. What if there's no truth to it? What if God is two-faced—shows one side to the rich and powerful, and the other to the losers of this world like myself?

My One-Night Stand is not so sure. "You know you're on the verge of a nervous breakdown," he tells me, "when you start to attribute the causes of your personal catastrophes to the spirit world." And maybe he's right.

A kiss is like a kick in the pants—it can wake you up. A kiss is disturbing if it's delivered at an inappropriate time. Or if the one kissing you will betray you—call you a whore or a bitch, or not call you at all. A kiss can wrap you up in bad feelings—be worse than pus oozing out of a neglected wound.

Kisses are like ants—they can crawl underneath your skirt and upset your equilibrium.

A man's body is a beautiful gift; a kiss is the gift wrapping. You can be decorated with medals or with kisses. I know what I would prefer, but I can't speak for war heroes or their widows. The sun and the moon battle for position; neither can claim victory. A kiss has power. It might not rekindle a dying star, but it can light your fire. Or break your heart.

The man I love bandages my wounds and says: "This wouldn't have happened if you had stayed with me."

And then I wake up and someone I don't know puts his foul tongue inside my mouth.

# Chapter 16

You don't go to a cemetery to visit the dead; you go to assure yourself that your loved ones can't possibly be here. When you enter a church or a temple, you don't expect anything out of the ordinary to take place. And yet in a cemetery you're always looking for a sign that your loved ones are in some magic kingdom. A house of life.

The Medieval writer, Edmund of Eynsham, claimed he saw the souls of the newly deceased ascend to the heavens in the form of sparks; his cousin, Thespesius, claimed he saw them as bubbles which rose and burst to disclose the forms of men and women.

Just before William Blake died, he told his wife, Catherine: "*My beloved, I am going to that country which I have all my life wished to see. I am happy, hoping for salvation through Jesus Christ. But we shall not be parted. I shall always be about you, to take care of you.*" I wish Dante had said something similar to me. But he said nothing. According to the police reports, he died instantly. His brother, Michele, who was in the car with him, noted there was no time for last words. No time for anything.

I wish the stone angel hovering over my husband's grave would wake up, flex his muscles, or shed a tear—anything would do.

I wish I would get a sign that my husband is alive and still loving me. I wish a passerby would stop and recite The Aztec Song of the Dead: *It ended with his heart transformed into a star. It ended with his journey to Death's kingdom with seven days of darkness. It ended with his body changed to light: a star that burns forever in that sky.* But no passerby stops and recites it. I am alone. I have the whole cemetery to myself.

Widows' tears flow easily, like rain. When it erupts, a volcano will kill thousands. Mother Nature has no feelings. Humans make up for it. Grief is like hot lava; if you don't get out of the way, it will definitely kill you.

Morphine dulls pain; grief needs something stronger—miracles.

When a man dies in Nepal, his widow writes his name on bamboo paper, and then burns it as an offering to the gods, all the time pleading with them: *Please don't let my dead husband return as a ghost. Please do not allow him to haunt me.*

I do no such thing. I want to be haunted. So on my bamboo paper, I write:

> *My dear friend, my dearest friend, my best friend, I miss you and must see you. The distance between us is too big. I can't come to you, so you come to me. Take any form you like.*
>
> *Soil needs rain; I need love—your love. Come and revive me.*
>
> *Your wife,*
> *Sophie Wolfe*

PART III

# Travel Guides

*Death is no more than the soul's passage*
*from one room to another.*

—WILLIAM BLAKE

# Chapter 17

"Oh my God, she's dead!" an ambulance attendant shouts, unable to find my pulse. Her face registers panic.

"Get the defibrillator," the doctor shouts. "She's in shock. She's haemorrhaging. She lost too much blood. Her heart stopped."

The ambulance attendants lack substance. I can see through them as if their clothes and skin were transparent.

I'm unconvinced the body lying in a pool of blood on my kitchen floor is mine. I try to get up, but can't.

I'm confused: Am I dead or not? If I am dead, how can I be thinking these thoughts? How can I exist?

The doctor frantically tries to revive me, pressing the pads against my chest—once, twice, three times. My body jumps in response.

"She's dead," repeats the ambulance attendant whose hair, I notice, is dyed. (I can see her roots.)

"Don't be so sure," he says. He once saw a corpse sit up in an autopsy room. When he started medical school, it was assumed oxygen starvation would cause irreparable brain damage in anything over six minutes, but it was now proven this was not always the case. In cold water, a person could survive for over 30 minutes, sometimes more, without oxygen. A French woman had been buried three days before she was revived by the shock of a grave robber cutting off her finger while trying to steal her ring. Eighteenth century doctors were constantly misdiagnosing the moment of death. Medical science had made advances; still, better to be safe than sorry.

The ambulance attendant puts her confidence in the doctor; he is older than she is. He's certain he can save me; why, I don't know. I don't even know if I want to be saved. I'm having too much fun listening in on people's conversations ...

Oh my God, I'm supposed to be having lunch with my mother. She'll wonder where I am, and why I'm late. I should have called her, but I dialled 911.

How can this be? I find myself floating a few feet above my body. The woman lying in the pool of blood was me, and now isn't me. The Medieval mystic, Caesarius of Hesterback, said: "*The soul is shaped like a glassy spherical vessel, with eyes before and behind, all-knowing and seeing everything at once.*" Is this what I am? It's hard to say. Have no time for such thoughts ... Good-bye, Sophie. It was nice sitting inside your skull, but now it's time for us to part. (Love you!)

Suddenly everything's dark. I am moving at great speed. I should be afraid, but I am not. Someone—a woman—takes me by the hand. Her hand feels like jelly. Oddly enough, it doesn't bother me. I sense my own hand has the exact same texture. I'm returning to my natural state, and this is the first of many changes.

The darkness is less complete now. A sun is rising on the horizon. Unlike our own sun, which can be harmful when you have too much of it, this sun can't hurt you. Its light has healing properties.

And then I notice Guido's grandfather. He's wearing a dazzling white shirt, and a pair of nice white pants with cuffs. He looks much younger and healthier than I ever remembered him to be.

"It's not your time," he says to me telepathically.

"He's right," says the woman whose hand I'm holding. "You still have a job to do."

I argue: I'm not about to change the course of history.

I'm shown a picture of a little girl. She has Dante's eyes. Suddenly, I have an overwhelming desire to return to my body.

You can stay if you want to, I'm told. "It's up to you."

I throw myself back into my body! Fuck, it hurts. The air feels heavy—like water. Fucking sea water.

A nurse rigs an IV bottle and puts a line into a vein in my arm; hooks a fucking tube in my mouth, in my nose; in my thoughts.

Edmund, a medieval monk and visionary, on being revived after having a near fatal heart attack, was so saddened by his re-entrance into this world that he yelled: "*O Holy Mary, for what sin do I lose so great a joy … truly was I well until this moment, but now I am truly ill.*" I can't say a word. I can't move. I can't concentrate.

Odd. There's a tube in my mouth, a tube in my nose, and an IV line in my arm and I don't feel a thing. The island of Montréal feels like a tiny room, and my hospital room feels like a cupboard I've been cornered in.

Odd. I'm haemorrhaging again and no one notices. Odd too I am losing all this beautiful blood and I weigh more now than I ever did. Someone should have told me dying has detrimental consequences.

When I wake up nothing is as I remembered it. I am in my hospital room, and I am not in my hospital room. The light streaming through the window has a fantastic hue. And it has substance. I put out my tongue and taste it. It's sweet, like *confetti*, Italian almond candies.

Sitting next to my bed is a woman of indeterminate age, wearing jeans and a white T-shirt.

"Do you have a name?" I ask.

"Of course I have a name. It's Gyorgy."

"Are you my guardian angel?"

"*Guardian angel* sounds so medieval. *Spirit guide*, New Age. Think of me as a travel guide. That might fit the bill."

"Am I in heaven?"

"Obviously not."

"Where am I?"

"Where am I?" she repeats.

I have often asked: "Who am I?" and not expected an answer. But I have never considered the question: "Where am I?" to be rhetorical.

Am I dead drunk or am I dead? Really dead?

Answers can be right or wrong, I'm told, but so can questions. In life, it's better not to ask: "Where are you?" but rather: "Where are you headed?" A world traveller seeks out the seven wonders; a trekker seeks to go where no one has gone before, but a psychic voyager demands more than cheap thrills.

If I want to meet my late husband, on his terms, on his turf, here's my chance. Call this life after life, or call it a miracle of self-deception: the road trip of a lifetime.

Both Inuit and Sioux shamans used music and dance to contact their spirit world; beating a drum is as good as a Christian or Buddhist prayer to get you in the spirit of things (pun intended) but it's not essential, I'm told telepathically.

In 1894, Black Elk, a Sioux, gave a detailed account of his journey into the Otherworld. He swore that he went through a door and the sun leapt at him and he heard it sing. Anyone, he believed, can cross the border between the two worlds, and see what he saw. All one needs is the desire to know things of the Otherworld.

A travel guide is not essential to be able to get to the Otherworld, but it helps, I'm told in Standard English.

"Actually, during the Middle Ages, Otherworld travels were common occurrences," Gyorgy lets me know. "Unfortunately, a lot of travellers falsified their reports to make themselves look better. Take Jacob Sprenger's *Malleus Maleficarum*. A nicely written horror story, but not much else. Even Dante Alighieri's *Divine Comedy* is full of errors. Small wonder few guides are now willing to escort the living across the border."

"The question is: will I have one?"

"Yes, but ..."

"But ...?"

"The Otherworld is a big place, Sophie. If you go to Africa, you can end up in the Sahara or in the Congo. And no matter where you land, what you see depends on your perspective. Ask ten photographers to take a picture of the same area, and not one picture will be the same."

The woman who calls herself Gyorgy—(what kind of name is that? Hungarian?)—sniffs the bouquet of flowers resting on my hospital night table. It is possible she is not an otherworldly visitor at all, but a caregiver my mother hired to take care of me.

"How are we going to get to this Otherworld?" I ask. Philo of Alexandria wrote that, at death, angels approach and greet the soul and invite it to mount a chariot which travels to a far-off place. But then he was a contemporary of Caesar. Anyone with clout had a chariot.

"You can go by plane or by ship—however, you like," she says. "Your world is a mirror image of ours. Actually, yours is the reflection, ours, the real thing. What you have, we have. When you cross over, you can immigrate (yes, immigrate!) to any country you like—France, Germany, Japan—it's up to you."

"Where's Dante?" That's all I'm interested in.

Dante's in Italy, she tells me, but where exactly, is anyone's guess. If she had a high-ranking position in the company she works for, she'd have access to the information, but she is at the bottom of the ladder. (Sorry.)

I pick up the phone and dial my travel agent's number.

Gyorgy laughs and tells me I don't need to dish out cash for this trip.

"In your world you have an idea, your idea has to be

translated into various steps," she explains. "But in our world, your thoughts do all the work. For example, in your world, if you want a new hairdo you go to the hairdresser and show her a picture of what you want, and she does it for you. In our world, you picture yourself in a new hair-do, and it's done. Call it thought-picture technology."

"Sounds like magic to me."

"On the contrary," she says. "It's basic science. Everything is made of light, you see. Your house, your clothes, your body, even the air you breathe can be broken down into its tiniest component, and it is light (in its various wavelengths). Light is your world's building blocks. And ours too."

And so?

"Light is easy to manipulate. Anyone can do it. All you need is the will."

"Show me," says doubting Thomas(ina).

My otherworldly visitor pulls out a laptop from her briefcase—(and to think I thought that's where she kept her wings!)—and shows me a map of the known universe.

She tells me: "Einstein theorized that if you increase the speed at which you're travelling, you can slow down time. (E.g., a twin travelling in a rocket will not age as quickly as his twin on earth.) Mind you, Einstein wasn't the first to figure out time changes depending on how fast you're moving, and where you are located in the cosmos. 2,500 years ago Buddhists calculated that 50 years in the human world are equal to one day and night in the Catum-maharajika heaven; in a Tavatismsa heaven 100 years in the human world are equal to one day and night. Einstein, of course, went a step further. He correctly theorized that, if you leave this world, the rules of common sense no longer apply."

I tell her: "I don't want a lecture. I want to find my husband. Let's go."

My travel guide seems to be in no hurry to leave. Opening the hospital window, she tells me: "The ancient Semites used to think of the world as a duplex: the sky-gods lived on the second floor (Heaven), humans were sheltered on the first floor (Earth), the dead were gathered in the basement, some parts of which were nicely finished (not such a bad place), and other parts were dark and unpleasant (Hell). The ancient Semites influenced the Jews; the Jews influenced the Egyptians and the Romans, and they in turn captured the imagination of the Christians."

So what is the woman saying? The universe can be compared to a big apartment building? The living occupy one floor, the dead another? Does each century have its own quarters or do individuals from various centuries inter-mix? Do the little guys rub shoulders with Kings and Queens? And is one able to take an elevator from one floor to the next and drop in for a visit? Milking the image for what it's worth: Do the dead go to the bathroom? And more importantly: Do the dead watch the living? And if they do, do they use satellites? Are concerns about privacy ever raised? (It doesn't seem right they should spy on us and we can't do likewise.) But then, if the universe is a big apartment building, does God own it alone or does he have shareholders? Do angels hold an interest in the real estate? What about the bad guys: do the devils get a piece of the action? Or are they absentee landlords?

If the universe is a big apartment building and the

living and the dead co-exist, can we opt for a co-op? Can we have a say in its direction? Do the rich have a larger controlling interest? Or do you have to have a large family (or better yet, a tribe) to have clout? If the universe is a big apartment building, do we have to pay rent? And if so, what do we pay it with? Are our pain and disappointments —currency? Or is it our happiness (our accomplishments) which count for something? If the universe is a big apartment building, can the landlord throw us out? According to one legend, He already has.

Gyorgy is unimpressed with my theological speculations.

"If you want to travel to the Otherworld, Sophie, you need an open mind. Get rid of your cynicism," she says. "Cynicism is akin to wearing someone else's eyeglasses. (They don't do you much good.) This is the Age of Cynicism and frankly, it annoys the hell out of me."

Think I: It doesn't look like my otherworldly travel guide will do much for me—except chat. Chat about everything, except what really matters.

"Tell me what God is like," I ask.

"What do you think God is like?" she replies as might a clinical psychologist working in *la Ville de Montréal.*

"When I'm happy," I say, "I fancy God is your average genie—He can make wishes come true. When I am not so optimistic about the powers of positive thinking, I fancy God to be like the president of a children's wish foundation. Praying is similar to a service request. We expect God to do as we ask. And we don't even pay the Guy. So if you put someone to work, and you don't pay him, the fellow is a slave. Only a slave would try to satisfy our enormous greed (would have no choice). Give me this, give me that. If God isn't a slave (unlikely He is), what is it we offer in exchange for his services? Admiration? Still, do our SOSs please the Old Guy or do they tire Him out? Some days I fear God isn't a genie or a slave but the boss of all bosses. Do as I say, or else!"

Again, my otherworldly visitor is unimpressed.

"In the Age of Cynicism," she says, "God can be anything and everything. Pity. Believe it or not God is taking a personal interest in what is happening on this planet. If humans make the evolutionary leap from Animal to Thinker to Compassionate Species, God will be pleased."

Enough talk.

I remove the IV tube hooked to my arm and manage to get out of the hospital bed. I put on my clothes, grab my purse and decide it's time to check out.

At the door (is it a door?), I am greeted by a *Woman of Shining Countenance and Bright Apparel.* Light is emanating from inside her body. It's ten times brighter than the sun but it doesn't hurt to look at it.

Is this God? Her eyes are kind.

The question is answered telepathically with a resounding: No.

Think I: Here's Mrs. Santa Claus and her merry elves.

*The Woman of Shining Countenance and Bright Apparel* is not pleased.

Cynics, she says, are no better than thieves; cynics steal what's unrightfully theirs. (What that is, she doesn't say.)

"A life review is no joking matter," she says. "It's the

event of the century. The be-all and end-all. Call it whatever you like."

Suddenly, her entourage (men in black) direct me to a conference room. (It has the look of an Imax theatre.) Here, on the various screens, different events in my life are delivered simultaneously. I see myself growing up (past and present interlap!)—my first steps, my first day at school (where's Daddy?), my first kiss, and my first major confrontation with my mother. Here I am at my 14th birthday party, opening a present and finding a toy horse with a note—a year's riding lessons, but it's not what I wanted. I watch myself throw the toy horse on the floor. I had wanted driving lessons, but my mother said No ... Suddenly I am made to feel the pain my mother experienced as I rejected her present; I am made to view the incident from her point of view; I am made (or allowed!) to understand that yes I was too young to learn how to drive.

More video clips are shown on screen, one after the other. Like a montage. The strange part is I don't feel invaded, or spied on; it's more like I am watching my own visual diary, except, I am now being given the chance or opportunity to perceive the events from other peoples' perspective!

I watch the drama enfold like I would a Shakespeare play—I know the plot beforehand. I don't judge the characters; I accept them as written. (Can't argue with Shakespeare.) Watching the video clips, I feel detached but interested in the drama presented; the events were played out according to the script. I didn't make any major errors (not really) and that knowledge (I am who I am, and that is good enough) produces an unexpected sense of euphoria.

*The Woman of Shining Countenance and Bright Apparel* continues to show me video clips of the events in my life. I am expected to evaluate them. But this is not a trial. When teachers review a student's progress, you don't call it a trial, do you? When you evaluate a painting on a wall, do you put it on trial?

"What have you done with your life?" asks *The Woman of Shining Countenance and Bright Apparel.* "What have you done to show us?"

My mind goes blank.

"She has a B.A. in Religious Studies," Gyorgy tells her.

"A dime a dozen," one of the men in black, the prosecutor, I gather, retorts.

"Whom did you love?" asks *The Woman of Shining Countenance and Bright Apparel.*

"Dante Aglieri, my husband. I did everything I could to make him happy," I tell her, but as soon as I say it, I wonder if it's true. I didn't have to do anything for him; he was the one doing things for me. He cleaned, he cooked, he ate me up till I had fantastic orgasms. I was the lucky one. Not he.

The prosecutor agrees with my assessment.

"Everyone loves their husbands, your Honour, especially the good looking ones," he tells *The Woman of Shining Countenance and Bright Apparel*, reminding those in the room that there are two ways an individual can speed up his application process to get to heaven—through Love (Charity) or through Knowledge. Love has more weight, but those who manage to contribute to a better understanding of the world also get preferential treatment.

Just then a police officer hurries into the room.

"Your Honour, there has been some clerical error," he says. "This woman, Ms Sophie Wolfe, should not be here. She is not dead."

"I thought this kind of thing only happened in our office in India," replies *The Woman of Shining Countenance and Bright Apparel.*

"What can I say, your Honour? It's not her time yet. As I said, she's not dead!"

*The Woman of Shining Countenance and Bright Apparel* is not amused.

How did I get here, she wants to know. Drugs? Sleeping pills? Suicide is not taken lightly. Like slapping the Creator in the face—gives you a nice gift, and you reject it.

"She didn't try to kill herself," Gyorgy assures her. "I brought her over."

*The Woman of Shining Countenance and Bright Apparel* looks at her sternly and tells her: "Temporary visas into the Otherworld are no longer issued. You must have known this?"

"Sophie Wolfe is a young widow. She was on a self-destructive path. I wanted to help her."

After a brief consultation with her entourage, *The Woman of Shining Countenance and Bright Apparel*, turns to Gyorgy and tells her: "I understand this is not the first time you broke the rules. Your relentless pursuit of your clients' interests has already cost you one demotion. Are you ready for another?"

"Yes," she says, unrepentant.

"I see," says *The Woman of Shining Countenance and Bright Apparel* and then turns to me and showers me with an unexpected dose of love and compassion.

"You had the misfortune of being assigned a travel guide whose work is under review. She's inept, but means well."

Pleads Gyorgy: "Your Honour, please let her stay and find her husband. She needs to learn whether or not he was murdered. You said yourself the universe has to be just for it to make sense."

"Okay, your client can stay for a while, but I expect her to recite the Honour Codes at our next meeting, and if she can't, she will never, ever be happy."

*The Woman of Shining Countenance and Bright Apparel* then claps her hands and she and her entourage leave. (Melt right into the wall, they do!)

Fact or fiction: When Orpheus looked for his dead wife, Eurydice, in the underworld, the furies in a moment of madness tore him limb from limb?

# Chapter 18

Driving through the Alps all I hear is the sound of my own breath. The woman sitting next to me is sound asleep. She might be a *bona fide* travel guide, or someone pretending to be one.

It is winter and it is cold. The weather is intolerable. The cold sticks to my skin like thistles.

The radio in my rented Ferrari won't make a sound. Even predators in the area don't show up and remind me there's life in these mountains. The Alps put me in my place. They're Sky Gods and I'm of no consequence. Ever since my husband died, I feel worthless. I am never sure of where I am, or rather, where I should be. I always feel lost.

At home, in Montréal, even when I was in my bed, I didn't feel comfortable. The size was all wrong. After the man I shared it with died, I felt I disappeared in it. Lost too much weight, I guess. Every night I would put on my flannel PJs like a soldier would put on a bullet-proof vest. I wore them for protection. Asleep, I wouldn't remember having had a husband and loving him and wanting him and needing him to warm me up. Asleep, I wouldn't remember my husband was murdered, or ask why. But then I would suddenly wake up and remember I had no one to talk to, no one to go out on long walks with. I would remember how much I hated watching movies by myself, eating by myself. The sitcoms did me no good. (Who was laughing? Not me!) The only thing I looked forward to was bedtime. That's when I would pull on my flannel PJs and hope my late husband would take them off in my dreams.

It is winter in Canada. Winter in Italy. Winter in my heart. It's as cold as ice and I'm confused. Am I in the Alps, or if I have fallen asleep, travelling inside my dreams, running red lights, courting danger? Possibly I am in Italy, taking a tour of the place; being on sick leave, I have ample time to zigzag through the Alps, zigzag through my own thoughts, chasing after wisdom, starving for it.

Am I in an imaginary car or a real one? Am I rolling up the car window because the wind is getting chilly, or am I getting chilly because I don't have a man to keep me warm? The temperature gets knocked down a few degrees every time you are reminded love is missing from your life.

What good are a pair of shoes if you can't wear them? What good are a pair of lips if you can't place them against someone else's lips and be assured a kiss is more than a hello/good-bye? It is an invitation to speak up, to be noticed, to be understood.

I had to leave home. My bed, without the man I loved in it, was less inviting than a cot inside a prison camp.

It's much better to be on the road, drive through the Alps, look up and think: a mountain is like a wedding cake, thin at the top, wide at the bottom, than to be at home and be reminded that no one is sharing your bed. A wedding cake whets your appetite for romance. That's why it's served at the end of the meal when the bride and groom can pack up and leave. (If one served it at the beginning, the sugary appetizer might chase the couple away.)

You don't have to live in Italy to believe in romance. Everyone has the right to a Silver Anniversary. I did too.

It's cold but I don't mind it all that much. It hurts less than grief. In the car's head unit I plug in music Dante downloaded for me. The tango (*Sonar Y Nadas Mas*) envelops me like a warm mist. I hear myself singing: "*Don't wake up if you're dreaming of love. To love is to dream. To wake up is to destroy the illusion. To wake up is to kill hope and to face the cruel reality, with nights of anxiety. That's why I want to dream because dreaming you'll never cry. Dream that he is yours, and he lives only for you. To dream, always to dream. While your soul catches a glimpse of the stars, you'll see that the world is happy. To dream is to live.*"

Am I driving in the Alps or am I asleep in my bed, dreaming I am? Are my eyes open or closed? Without the man I love my eyes could just as well be glued shut.

When I was a little girl I asked my mother: "Why do people die?"

"The answer lies beyond the limits of *your* intelligence," she told me. Or did she say: "The answer lies beyond the limits of *our* intelligence?"

If I had paid more attention, I might not have judged her so harshly, and in turn, I might now not be judged ...

I asked my second grade teacher the same question: "Why do people die?" The best answer she knew of, she said, was found in an Algonquin legend. She took a picture book with the legend in it and read it to me:

> *Years ago when the world was new, the First Mother and the Grand Chief's nephew fell in love and had lots of children but no food.*
>
> *"What shall we do?" asked the Grand Chief's nephew, and the First Mother replied: "Kill me. Tear my flesh from my body and bury it. Wait seven moons and then when you return, you will find the food you need."*
>
> *The Grand Chief's nephew did not want to kill her, but she insisted. Seven moons later, just as she had said, on the spot where her flesh had been strewn, there was corn. She gave her life so her family might live and flourish.*

The tale of self-sacrifice did not answer the question for me. I told the teacher as much. I can still remember the sad look on her face.

# Chapter 19

Asleep, you travel outside the boundaries of civility. Often, you don't behave. You shoot your mouth off. You fuck around and take pleasure in it. You celebrate the id. Like driving blindfolded on a dare and surviving it unscathed—that's sleep for you. Travelling through the Otherworld has the same quality to it, I'm told.

"Your world is a mirror image of our own," explains my travel guide. "Except, every square inch of our world is divided into six spheres or planes. Actually, divided is the wrong word. Each city or town co-exists on six different spheres or planes. Once you pass into our world, you can choose to live in any country you like, but the sphere or plane you're allowed to go to is determined by our archons or gatekeepers. Better believe it, what you did in your lifetime counts. You can't have a universe which makes sense and not have a justice system in place. Mind you, eternal damnation is not anyone's idea of fair play. In our world everyone gets a second chance. Upward mobility (the right to go to a higher plane of existence) is more or less guaranteed. All you have to do is respect the Honour Codes and you're on your way."

Turning right on the *autostrada*, my travel guide and I soon find ourselves in Venice. But it's not the Venice Hollywood has made popular. This city is ugly. Large parts of it have sunk into the lagoon. The Venetian waters are murky. The skies appear just as filthy. I didn't think clouds could have grease stains till now.

It's hard to say which sphere or plane we're presently in, but whatever it is, the place is not one anyone in their right mind would want to end up in. The stench of the motor oil fumes makes me nauseous.

My travel guide and I try to book a room at a hotel, but the staff can't attend to us. Everyone is sick.

The manager, an asthmatic, tells us: "I wouldn't have been sent to this hell hole (cough), had the company I so eagerly worked for on the mainland not knowingly contributed to air pollution. I could have used my position (cough) as a chief executive officer (cough) to limit the damage, but I didn't. My inaction put Venice's 847 frescoes, 4,000 bas reliefs, 7,000 sculptures, 105 churches and 2,000 oil paintings in jeopardy. Petrochemical emissions are pouring 15,000 tonnes of sulphuric acid a year over Venice, and nothing is being done."

"Pity," says my travel guide. "The Mafia has an Honour Code. So does the Planet Earth. Abide by its code, and *The Good Life* is yours. Break it, and all hell breaks loose."

Italy's topography is complex. Gyorgy can't find her way around. If she were a fully accredited otherworldly travel guide, she would have a GPS and full access to her company's satellite service, but for a number of reasons, she hasn't been able to move up the ranks.

The question sneaks up in my mind: Am I travelling with an inept travel guide or a con artist?

I ask the woman in the car with me: "Why were you demoted? You don't have a criminal record, do you?"

She hesitates before she replies. "I prefer to think of those I help as my friends, rather than as my clients. This is considered unprofessional. I am not supposed to become emotionally involved. Psychologists manage it, so should I. But I can't do it. I become attached, and take risks. This doesn't sit well with the upper echelons."

"I see," I say, but I don't.

The industrial City of Milan looms ahead. Its massive skyline advertises this is the real capital of Italy. Business thrives here. Bankers, fashion designers, publishers, and men and women with an axe to grind can all be found in the centre of town hiding out in their office buildings, waiting for the right moment to move on to a higher plane—a better job, a better house, a better world all-around.

The traffic on the *autostrada* becomes heavy and oppressive; the drivers are tired and irritated. In the next lane I catch a glimpse of a woman and a man arguing. In the back seat, a poodle with a tiara strapped to its head.

It took a while to understand how this Otherworld operates. First, in the lower spheres or planes, thought-pictures don't work. You can't imagine a car, and presto, there it is. You have to buy or rent one. (We did.) In this super-terrestrial region individuals learn the way of all flesh, or rather of all spirit, ascending or descending, depending on their noted progress. The higher planes resemble an idyllic version of reality. The lower ones resemble humans' worst nightmares. Each plane or sphere contains many different levels or "telonies." You can't go from one level to the next without a guide.

Fashions come and go. And so do ideas. Each generation re-designs the afterlife—offering a new and improved architectural blueprint. And yet, the basic structure remains faithful to the original design. (The good are rewarded; the bad, punished.)

At noon, in the heart of the business district, crowds of people are hurrying from one building to the next; the pace is so frantic, just watching them makes me anxious.

"Relax," says my guide, but she herself doesn't look relaxed.

At the first opportunity, she parks the car. In Milan the rich flaunt their good fortune, and the poor don't hide at home watching TV. They're on the streets, shouting obscenities and curses at passersby.

A man in a loincloth stops and tells us his story. He was at one time the president of a large automotive company, but then he was accused and convicted of defrauding his shareholders. Now he owns nothing, except for his alms bowl and his clothes. He begs for his meals. He's a wanderer without a home, sleeping at night under a tree or in a shelter.

If someone can tell him what the poor are most in need of, he will be released from his fate.

Money is offered.

"The poor don't need your pity," he says, but he takes the money anyway.

"How ungrateful," I say.

Gyorgy gives me an earful. Why should the poor thank the rich for what is rightfully theirs? As St. Ambrose of Milan noted: "The rich man who gives to the poor does not bestow alms, but pays a debt."

"Honour thy poor," I acknowledge, thinking myself clever.

"You didn't learn a thing," says my travel guide. "In a world as wealthy as yours, no one should be poor."

I look at my watch. No time to solve riddles. I have to find my husband.

That's it—what the poor are most in need of is time.

Right, but wrong, I'm told. The rich need time as much as anyone else.

"The rich no more deserve to be rich," says my travel guide, "than the poor deserve to be poor. Anyone who has more than another should demand forgiveness of the one who has less."

My travel guide hails a limousine and the former VIP steps into it, a free man.

If my travel guide answered the question asked—what the poor are most in need of, I failed to catch it.

"A question has more than one answer," she tells me, and leaves it at that.

The road we're on meanders, and suddenly, we're in Assisi. I enter a fabric store on *Via Roma* in a nondescript town and ask for directions. At the counter is a man whose name tag identifies him as Francis Bernardone.

"The salesclerk shares the same birth name as St. Francis of Assisi, Italy's patron saint," I tell my travel guide.

"What of it?" she asks.

"Don't you see the irony in it? St. Francis may have loved birds (as much as he loved to striptease) but he detested his parents for making their living working in the rag trade. Basically, St. Francis divorced his parents and had himself adopted by the Holy Roman Catholic Church. If there was ever a bad son in the history of human(un)kind, he is it! St. Gregory the Great believed souls endure their Purgatory in the very places in which they sinned."

My travel guide is unimpressed with my theological summation. She reminds me:

*a) We're not in Italy to do psychological autopsies on Italy's beloved saints and,*
*b) Legends are more valuable than life histories.*

Then it hits me—loving one's parents is sometimes next to impossible, but anyone (even a little critter like myself) should be able to honour them!

Torino's east-end industrial park looks like any other on the continent: polluted, overcrowded, and glum. The place isn't overrun with oversized rats and dragon lizards and club-footed monsters or lakes of fire but this is not a place that one would want to call home.

A run-down shoe factory on *Via Firenze* supposedly has a worker by the name of Dante Aglieri. The place is poorly lit, and smells like a manure pit. Employees are hit on the head if they don't work fast enough. The foreman tells us the assembly line is made up of CEOs who knew their workers were being poorly treated and chose not to do anything about it. While they earned over a million a year, their workers were paid less than $1.60 a day.

"It looks like the Otherworld is into vendettas," I say.

The foreman is not pleased. "Anyone can endure the rigours of chastisement," he says, "if it is known the stay is temporary. No one stays here forever. Call this a place of purification or expiation or rehabilitation, just don't call it hell."

My guide agrees. "Anything is bearable, if you know it won't last forever."

I don't have time for another morality play. I am looking for my husband and he can't be here because he didn't exploit anyone.

"Didn't your husband wear shoes?" asks the foreman. "Were they Nike? Gap? Levis? Or Strauss?"

If this man is going to lecture me on "Consumers' Responsibilities," I'm going to scream. Got a bellyful from my mom. She is forever going around saying consumers should campaign to improve conditions for workers whose products they use. (But what does she do about it—except buy, buy, buy?)

Animals in the jungle can walk around barefoot (one big kitchen), but the urban jungle poses a lot more danger to man(un)kind.

A bell rings. A screen pops up. On it appear the words of the Sicilian ballad, "A Lament for the Death of Turiddu Carnivali." The workers belt out:

*There is a law which doesn't fail.*
*Bread to the empty stomach.*

*Clothes to the naked.*
*Water to the thirsty.*
*And Honour and Liberty to the one who works.*

My travel guide joins in and wins a standing ovation. The woman has the voice of an angel; I don't.

# Chapter 20

Italy changes to suit your mood. It becomes what you want it to be. Its people conspire to make your trip a big success—telling you whatever you want to hear. If you're after veal *scallopini*, they'll serve it to you and declare it their national dish; if you're a vegetarian, they'll dress up your dish with zucchini flowers, and swear the eating of flesh is barbaric and should be outlawed. In Italy, what you see is not what you get. You have to go to the United States for that.

Travelling by car through Italy is a great way to see the country. This country is not one country but dozens. You find below freezing temperatures in the knee-cap and the Sahara in the calf. You find light-skinned and dark-skinned people speaking in dialects as foreign to each other as French is to English. Historical time zones also vary. One minute you're in a medieval hill town, the next, you're lost in a city as modern as New York. And yet, wherever you go, everyone's warm and friendly and ready to chat. Call Italy a nation of diplomats.

In Italy's small towns you don't have to be a celebrity to be appreciated. Everyone knows everyone else—you don't need a gossip columnist or a *People Magazine.* You don't even need a family name, a nickname will do. Actually, the larger commercial centres in Italy also give you that small town feeling. (Everyone knows your name—Cheers to you!) First of all, most cities and towns look alike. And second of all, anywhere you go in Italy you'll find the same street names. You'll find a *Via Firenze* and a *Via Roma* anywhere and everywhere.

Street signs can tell you as much about a country as its literature. In Québec, *La Belle Province,* where the majority of people speak French, if you put up a sign in English, you spook the population. That's why the language police was created. (They're ghost busters!) In New York City streets are given numbers which say something about the money capital of the world. The mighty buck rules in Italy too, except no one's singing its praises.

"Keep your eyes on the road," my travel guide reminds me, and I do as she says. Her presence assures me I'm not in Hell, because, Hell, as everyone knows is a dark pit called Loneliness. It can be found anywhere—even in one's own backyard.

Medieval scholars often compared Earth to a prison where you had to do your time before you could be set free (in Heaven); a few even suggested Earth was Purgatory, an intermediate state between Heaven and Hell. Nowadays, Earth is often compared to a big school in which students are supposed to learn how to love. (My mom's pet theory.)

"Any species which stockpiles nuclear weapons can't forgive and forget," I tell my guide. "Hate is part of our heritage. Dogs are naturally better at making love (not war) than Man, so why is it that Man is made in God's image? If your teacher is a real dog, now you know why. Scholars ought to consider comparing the Earth to a dog house."

"Continue to be a cynic," she says, "and you'll never get laid again."

Ouch ...

"I imagine in Heaven everything is in mint condition," I say, but it's more of a question than a statement. "In Heaven do buildings rise out of the ground as do ferns? Everything can renew itself?"

"Comparing Earth to Heaven is like comparing being healthy to being sick," she says.

Yes, but what I would like to know is do children in Heaven age? Do they go to school? Or do they spend their time playing?

"I imagine kids in Heaven are like kids anywhere," she says. "As most take a natural pleasure in learning, they probably attend school and learn to do things for themselves. Their teachers help them develop at their own pace, bringing out their natural capacities, stimulating their senses and thinking. There is no danger of being spoiled. Children can have as much fun as they like."

"Do children have direct access to the Divine?" I ask. "When a child dies does he bypass the in-between worlds and go straight to Heaven? I suspect Catholics wrongly assume unbaptized children are housed in Limbo, on the fringe of Hell. God, an advocate of mercy and compassion, would not condemn innocents, would He?"

"Legend has it God resides in the *Coelum Empyreum*, outside the six spheres, above the ninth heaven, but that's all I know. Heaven and Hell are restricted areas."

In a just society everyone gets a chance to move up; in an unjust one Lady Luck rules.

In San Remo, the largest otherworldly gambling resort on the Italian Riviera, body parts are what you play with. The amputations are swift and painless.

Entering a gaudy casino, a disembodied head with the words, *in coelum ascendum*, tattooed on his cheeks, asks: "Was your husband in the Mafia?"

"Not that I know of," I say.

"I was," he admits. "A police officer shot me in the back."

"I'm sorry," I say, though it's hard to feel sorry for a Mafia thug. Drug traffickers, car thieves, kidnappers, loan sharks, blackmailers and hit men don't inspire compassion.

Flashing on the ceiling of the gaudy casino are the words of the ancient Chinese philosopher, Lao-Tzu: "*If a man shall do me wrong, I will offer in return my full love. The greater the injury he attempts, the greater must be the offerings I offer in return.*"

On the tiled floor are the words of the Buddha: "*Hate Not, Even your Enemy.*"

My travel guide turns to me and says: "You can't leave this hell hole, unless this Mafia hit man does as well."

# Chapter 21

The road meanders through large wooded areas; sometimes we come across ancient Roman fortress towns, and other times, big cities.

"Drive on," says my travel guide. "You're not going to find your husband here." I notice, on the side of the road, a hairy female beating an old man with a stick. How can this be? And then it hits me: you can have Heaven or Hell in the same geographical area. Even on my little island in Montréal, enter one house and there's joy; enter the one next to it, there's grief. This world co-exists on many levels as does our own. For life's journey you don't take a boat or a train. Our bodies are the vehicles we drive in. Once you come through the birth canal, there's no turning back. You have to sit through Year One, Year Two, etc.; with each stop your perception changes. You don't even have to get out of your body-vehicle to enjoy the different sights. Young eyes, cocky eyes, wise eyes—all kinds of lenses are provided through the years to filter the information. And you can't say you've seen it all till cataracts interfere with the view. Could be all the action is taking place inside the body-vehicle itself, but what interests us the most always seems to be taking place elsewhere ...

"For the universe to make sense, it should be fair," the woman I'm travelling with insists yet again, adding: "Christianity envisages a judgement with Heaven, Hell or Purgatory as the soul's destination. Hell and Purgatory address the need for retribution. Our century is noted for: fast foods, fast girls, instant gratification, instant coffee, instant therapy: heaven-in-a-cup. Sin has lost its allure. (Like, you're not a bad girl, you're sick—or your mommy was.) Intermediate states are out of fashion. Heaven is yours for the asking. Would it be so!"

"I'm not a Christian," I say.

She continues: "Buddhism gives no promise of an eternal life but it too envisages a judgement. For every soul a protracted, but not endless cycle of reincarnations, each determined by his karma."

*Sow figs, reap figs.*
*Sow kindness, and reap it in the next life.*
*Sow hate, and you reap it.*

"I'm not Buddhist," I say.

"No problem," she says. "All religions are one."

"Tell that to the Pope."

"Intermediate states (Purgatory for lack of a better word) are out of fashion," she repeats, "but that doesn't make them any less valid."

I tell her: "Well, if one is looking for an in-between

world where everyone gets what's coming to them, Italy is the best place to find it. In a Protestant country like Germany one would be laughed off the stage (or road). Most Germans believe the soul ascends directly into Heaven or descends into Hell. (A German God can't be wishy-washy.) Italians, on the other hand, love two things: cutting cards and cutting deals. Purgatory offers the best of both worlds—you can be bad, and get away with it. Actually, any foreign country, whether you're a tourist or a political refugee, is an in-between world. You're there to regain your sense of balance or direction. Back home I couldn't eat or sleep, forever worried I would be a victim of foul play. Strangely enough, in Italy, a Mafia stronghold, I feel safe."

"Good," she says. And leaves it at that.

In Italy it seems everyone's on a religious pilgrimage. Some are in search of miracles, but the majority are simply looking for a shoulder to cry on. As this world has failed them, it's the Otherworld on which they pin their hopes. They'll climb steep cliffs and enter dark caverns to pay homage to their favourite saints. It doesn't matter if a pilgrim's prayers are answered or not because, once you're on the road, you'll inevitably find out you're not alone; everyone has a problem, some worse than yours, and that can't but do you good.

Italians accept suffering; it's part of life. Rather than deny its importance, or nullify it, they seek out the spirit world. In Italy the most important entertainments of the year are those which celebrate the feast days of the saints and of the Mother of Christ, which makes me draw the conclusion that the entire peninsula is a sanctuary for anyone who has lost a loved one or is nursing a broken heart.

In Italy you're allowed to wear your heart on your sleeve. You're allowed to grieve over the loss of a loved one—there's nothing unnatural about it. In North America grieving is a no-no. In North America you are not supposed to suffer because, if you do, you're considered mentally ill. Pills are pushed on those who don't feel good —"Come on, be normal—put on a happy face."

Italians are not a happy people. Nor are North Americans for that matter. The difference between Italians and North Americans is that Italians accept unhappiness is part of life and North Americans don't. North Americans believe everyone has the right to happiness, and should aim for it. For Italians happiness is a non-issue. What's important is to acquit oneself with honour: to do the right thing, to be of service to others, to love one's family and to provide for them. Having fun is at the bottom of the To-Do-List. It's not that Italians don't love fun and adventure, they do, but they don't perceive it as the end-all and be-all of existence. For Italians unhappiness can be a blessing in disguise. It can lead to enlightenment.

That's why I'm here—in a rented car, driving through Italy—I can look for my dead husband and not be put in the loony bin. I can roll down the car window and sing at the top of my lungs the lyrics to the tango, *Quiero Verte Una Vez Mas,* and not be thought a fool. Or a madwoman. If my voice is not up to par, it does not matter. This is a prayer: "*I need to see you one more time. I am so sad. I can't remember why you left. In my grief I searched for you without finding you. Fever burns my senses. I need to see you one more time to relieve my torment or I die. There is no forgetting you. I must see you one more time.*"

A village perched on a knoll draws my attention.

Donkeys, cream-coloured oxen, cows, bulls, goats, pigs and chickens roam the cobbled streets unattended.

"Nothing is as it seems," says my travel guide.

I stop the car and head for the Central Registrar's office.

After I tell the Archon or gatekeeper my story the woman assures me my husband can't possibly be here. Her village is reserved for those who dishonoured their partners.

"Like adulterers," I say.

"Oh please," she says, "it's never that simple."

A woman dressed like a pig enters the room on all fours.

"Can I have the key?" asks the woman in pig's clothing.

The Archon lifts the piggish woman's skirt and procures it.

"The bathroom's to your left," she tells her.

And to me she says: "Had not this woman falsely accused her ex-husband of child abuse, the key would have fit the lock in Heaven's Gate."

# Chapter 22

In Tuscany the air is warm and nicely scented. At the beginning of my trip, in the Alps I wore heavy clothing, it felt like I had a heavy carpet round my shoulders, but here, I can go out in a T-shirt and jeans.

Every little town we stop in has its own style of cooking. Some offer pastas with cream sauce; others toss it with olive oil, Parmesan cheese, herbs and a variety of dried fruits and nuts. They're to die for. Only in Italy can you put on weight and be unconcerned about it. In North America fasting is seen as a form of self-discipline; in Italy, self-flagellation.

I'm hungry and I'm happy. Happiness increases my appetite. Travelling increases my appetite. Soul-searching increases my appetite. And I've had more than my share of the above ...

Next stop: Florence. The great city unmasks my ambitions. Yes sir, I am very ambitious, I can admit it now. Anyone who wishes herself happiness is ambitious and a damn fool and deserves what's coming.

Walking in and out of the city's churches and palaces, I take in the sites, hoping to find Dante, my beloved husband.

Quite a few storekeepers gawk at me, as if I were a wild animal on the loose. Like, where's my name tag? (Everyone has one dangling from their left ear.) And what's with my clothes? (Compared to theirs, mine look dull and heavy.)

A local artisan calls the authorities. The men, dressed like papal Swiss guards, waste no time in apprehending me.

My travel guide shows them her I.D. and suddenly they're full of apologies. They bow to her, and to me too. I now know what a commoner feels when she marries into royalty.

A woman offers me her parasol—as a gesture of good will. Why? Because I'm travelling with an otherworldly guide. If you're with one, you can go anywhere you like. You can go from one sphere or plane to another—no questions asked.

In the main piazza I notice an open-air concert of Mozart's *Don Giovanni*. The music is the same, but different. More majestic somehow.

Otherworld musicians are always experimenting, I'm told; they like to surprise their audience. Their variations add spice.

"Don't be fooled," says my guide. "There are many Florences. Dante could be in any one of them."

"Shh," someone says, then notices my guide and blushes, embarrassed.

Travel guides (even low level ones) are a step higher than anyone else. As long as I'm with one, no one will challenge my right to look for Dante.

"What am I doing at the opera? I want to find my husband," I tell my guide.

"You have a point," she says, getting up, and immediately asking the locals questions about the whereabouts of a certain Dante Aglieri.

"Everyone knows where he is," says a driver of a horse-drawn carriage, and points to a café down the street.

The café is called "*Chez* Dante." It has a big sign in the window: "No Travel Guides Allowed."

Gyorgy encourages me to check up the place on my own, and I do.

Inside, I'm greeted by a young waitress dressed in a miniskirt and fringed blouse (ca. 1970s). No one else though opts for this fashion period; most of the patrons sport Renaissance clothing.

"I'm looking for Dante Aglieri," I tell her.

"Don't fret," she says, fingering her ear tag, "he'll be here any minute now."

The waitress' name tag is one of the longest I have ever seen—one loop after another—it reaches right down to her waist. She notices my interest and immediately removes it from her ear.

"Read it if you like," she says, and only then do I realize that this name tag (ear tag actually as it dangles from the ear like an earring) contains an individual's biography—important dates (birth, death), family pictures, etc.

I don't have the time to read it. All I want to know is whether her ear tag is as long as it is because she had more than one life? Because if she did, then it would prove Buddhists and Hindus are right about reincarnation—no one dies, everyone is re-born. Pope Anastasius IV issued a decree of anathema against anyone who believed in reincarnation or what he termed, "monstrous restoration," back in the 12th century. Ever since belief in reincarnation has been regarded as heretical among Catholics and Protestants alike. Those who believe in it can be excommunicated. Souls of the departed are supposed to pass directly to the Otherworld. (No turning back!)

I ask the waitress: "Is reincarnation the real deal? Is an individual's fate determined by the karma or ethical conduct followed in his previous life? Is it really true—each one of us is born again and again?"

"I only had one life that I remember and it was spent in Hollywood, California," she says. "I can't tell you if one is re-born after one leaves this place. I'm a newcomer myself, though I don't think anyone here actually knows or I would have been told. This much I do know—this world is an intermediate one. Everyone—man, woman and child (and everything else too—animals, plants, whatever)—has to pass through here before they reach the next world. (What that is, is anyone's guess.) One can stay here several centuries, or a few hours. An individual is expected to distil his memories; understand the significance of his past life, what he has learned and what he failed to learn."

Like I'm in Purgatory? For real? How medieval.

"Not exactly," says the waitress. "Listen, you don't have to be a Catholic to believe in an in-between world. Buddhists believe the soul can't move from one life to the next without an intermission. Think of this world as a commercial break."

The question is: am I in a super-terrestrial region, real or imaginary? Am I outside or inside space-time? In a six-dimensional world, opposed to our three-dimensional one?

It doesn't matter, I decide. I'm here to find my husband.

"There's your Dante," says the waitress pointing to a man in medieval garb walking in through the door.

A Dante, yes, but not my Dante! This man, whose image I have seen often enough on the internet, must be the author of, "The Divine Comedy." It's not whom I have been desperately looking for and possibly risking my life for. Not at all.

Tears stream down my cheeks. I can't help myself.

"Don't cry," says the waitress. "If you have some poetry to show Mr. Dante Alighieri, he'll take a look. He's a good fellow. He could have left this place and ascended to a higher sphere years ago, but he's chosen to stay. Go ahead. Introduce yourself."

Her tone shows no deference for the great man of letters; she could be pointing out a janitor or a carpenter. In this world everyone is given equal treatment. (Travel guides alone are shown deference.)

"Yes," agrees the telepath, "everyone is equal here. If folk weren't, can you imagine the commotion? Florence is chockfull of famous people. If a fuss were made every time a celebrity passed by, the place would be unbearable. In your world the rich put up fences and think themselves clever, safer; but if you want to be safe, it's best everyone is equal. Like on the beach—same sun, same amount of sunlight."

Removing her apron, answering questions I haven't even asked, she informs me in a breathless tone of voice that yes, the ancient Romans, Greeks, Egyptians (kings, slaves anyone and everyone) can be found in the vicinity. No cave men though—after 3,000 years folk have to move on.

"Listen," I say, "I'm looking for my husband, Dante Aglieri. I don't care to meet the famous wordsmith."

"Oh," she says, disappointed.

The waitress calls the assistant manager; the assistant manager calls the manager; the manager calls over the chef who immediately apologizes for the mistake. Everyone who comes to Florence wants an audience with the famous poet, Dante Alighieri.

"A poem should be consumed like a fresh slab of home-made bread," the chef says. "You have to be hungry, before you put it in your mouth."

The waitress doesn't agree; she would rather poetry be compared to a favourite sweet or liquor. Poetry—Dante's or anyone else's—should not be forced down one's throat. Because if it is, it turns poisonous, unfit for human consumption.

That's all well and good, but my own interest is: Does Dante Alighieri's *Divine Comedy* provide an accurate description of the Otherworld? Will its layout (Hell, an abyss; Purgatory, a conical-shaped mountain on an island in the Southern hemisphere) help me find the man I love?

"As a factual map of the heavens his *Comedy* is full of holes," admits the chef. "One shouldn't confuse poetry with information."

He adds: "Besides no one blames Mr. Alighieri for his inaccurate conclusions. In his time he was a progressive thinker, unlike some of his contemporaries."

He hands me a dessert menu. It's then I notice he has a striking resemblance to Dante. My Dante. The man is truly a hunk.

The chef suggests any of the Tuscan treats on the dessert menu would be good to eat, but he recommends a fruit salad, topped with whipped cream and pomegranate seeds. "It's light and fresh. And nutritious."

A man's concern for your well-being can be a powerful aphrodisiac.

"I can't have dessert," I tell him. "I promised myself I would not have any sweets until I find out who killed my husband."

"Don't worry," he says. "You don't have to order food. You can order a good book."

On the menu: Canadian classics like *The Edible Woman*, *Stone Angel* and *Bear.* Vitamins for the body, vitamins for the mind.

Every book ever written, published or unpublished, I'm told, sits on the shelves of his restaurant.

I ask if William Blake's lost manuscripts are available? No other poet or artist has had so much of his work destroyed or censored after his death.

The waitress immediately goes into the kitchen (library?) and brings out many manuscripts—so many, there is no way I could read them all.

She puts one of William Blake's unpublished plays under my nose. "Take a good sniff," she says.

I can't believe my eyes/ears—nose! One sniff and I read the play, which is as long as *Macbeth*.

The waitress explains that the more books you sniff, the taller you get. Knowledge is this world's drug of choice. Unfortunately few have time for leisure reading. Everyone has to work.

"People have to work?" I ask. And I thought in this world, what you want, is what you get?

"Everyone has to be of use," the waitress says. The universe is expanding. Lots of stars being born; lots of new planets are coming up for colonization. Plants, animals, eco-systems need to be designed. And maintained. Quite a challenge. Anyone who is willing to work, can.

I can't wait to tell my mother about this place. Give her work and she's in heaven.

A waiter brings the soup of the day to Mr. Alighieri. It smells so good ... I get a strong whiff of how it was for me and Dante ... Dante in the kitchen; my Dante, in the laundry room, washing his socks (and mine). That's what I long for the most—everyday things. Going to the corner store for milk together. Going to the park to watch kids run around, doing nothing and liking it. Sharing a joke. A meal. A movie. And all that jazz.

"I don't have time to read books or chat," I tell the waitress. "I have to find my husband."

Just as I'm about to leave the café, I notice the famed Italian poet has donned an apron and is now acting as the head waiter, taking orders. The manager is serving the waitress who is now sitting at my table, enjoying a strawberry cheese cake. I would give anything for one. Anything—but the chance to see my Dante.

# Chapter 23

Come spring the weather is warm and pleasant in Southern Italy. Little drops of happiness fall from the sky; you can collect it like rain. In Southern Italy you'll find an endless supply of blue skies, clean beaches, spectacular mountain vistas, fabulous wheat fields, fabulous corn fields, olive and grape orchards, beautiful sheep on the loose (won't give you the right of way) and costumed shepherds on the loose; you will also find unsmiling shopkeepers who won't sell you a thing unless you stay and talk for a while.

In Naples, every shop, every building, every doorstep has pots of smiling flowers, and on almost every street corner you'll find a musician, strumming a guitar. Fabulous boutiques and open air markets and five star restaurants and mouth-watering *gelaterie* make this the place to be. It wouldn't surprise me if Naples inspired the ancient Roman scribe, Tibullus, to describe Heaven as the Land of Endless Love.

The palm trees lining the roads make me think of Victorian grand duchesses. They'll shade you from the sun.

All you have to do is stop and pay them a few compliments. Get under their lacy green parasols, and you're set for life.

Italy's Amalfi coast offers more than spectacular views; it offers reassurance—I'm not losing my mind. I'll soon be back home, at work, in control, satisfied the world contains enough to sustain my curiosity. You can't go off the deep end if you're eager to find out the truth about things. Too much is at stake. The warm sea air fans my drive—you can do it, Sophie. You can find out who killed your husband. Be optimistic, and the future's yours.

A few days ago my fingers felt amputated. Today, I have no use for winter garments. I can put them in a CARE package and send them to my poor cousins in Canada. Okay, I don't have any cousins, but if I did, I would send them my mitts and virgin wool dunce cap ...

"Don't be lulled into a false sense of security," says my guide. "You came to Italy for a reason."

"You're right," I say. "I came here to find out who killed my husband. As you said, if the universe is to make sense, it must be just."

"Exactly," she says, adding something about everyone having a conscience; stamped on it: moral imperatives. "Most people can list Moses' Ten Commandments. The Buddha's Five Precepts are less well-known. If you can list them your IQ is probably higher than average."

"I did know them," I say, but no more.

She lists them for me:

*To abstain from taking life*
*To abstain from taking what is not given*
*To abstain from sexual misconduct*

*To abstain from false speech*
*To abstain from intoxicating things which cloud the mind*

"Are Moses' Ten Commandments, the Buddha's Five Precepts and the Honour Codes moral imperatives?" I ask. "And if they are, do they hold equal weight?"

"Not exactly," she answers, looking at me strangely. Am I mentally challenged, or what?

I tell her: "Faust bargained with the Devil: 'Give me the good things in life and when I die you can have my soul.' A contract was signed. God doesn't bargain. God says: 'Take life as is (without the perks my rival might throw in) and when you die you'll be nicely rewarded.' It's expected that both God and the Devil will honour their word. Honour is not about good or evil. (Even the Mafia has an Honour Code.) Honour is all about ego. Vanity. Self-engrossment. Italians have a long list of dos and don'ts. You can't do this or that or you'll dishonour the family name. And if you do, watch out! Honour is Italy's national obsession. Call it the disease of the millennium."

"You got it all wrong," my guide says. "Honour has nothing to do with self-importance. Or self-inflation. Honour is about civility. Being group-minded. Putting the needs of the many before the needs of the one. Cicero, the Roman orator, believed that the ideal candidate for heaven was not the ascetic who renounced the active life, but rather the statesman and public benefactor—the Man and Woman of Honour."

So?

"Be honourable and you prove you're less like an ant

or a beetle, and more like a super creature. Call it evolution. Call it progress. Call it a good thing. Just do it. Be honourable and, even if you don't save the world, you might just save your ass."

"You think you know it all, but you don't," I say, annoyed.

"A paradigmatic sage is not only a teacher but a learner," she replies, quoting someone or other.

"Why is there so much needless suffering in the world?" I ask. "So much loneliness? Poverty? Needless child deaths? Needless wars?"

She recites the Honour Code: Honour thy planet, honour thy workers, honour they partners, honour thy parents, honour thy children, honour thyself ...

"Anyone can rattle off an Honour Code," I tell her. "But it's not the answer to what I asked."

"Virtue can be learned," she says. "Anyone can become a sage, a person of humble rank or of high rank, but it takes time."

"I don't need platitudes. I need love."

# Chapter 24

And then I turn around and there, in front of a little house on a hill totally covered in flowers, is the man I have been looking for. I know him like I know my own skin. My own thoughts.

Here is the place where those who have said good-bye are re-united, they return and hear the beat of their hearts, and in the distance, the beat of the tango (*Una Piba Como Vos*): "*Life is beautiful and flattering; it is eternal spring if by your side you hear your lover's voice. The flowers smile at you when you walk, with pleasure, arm in arm. The wind caresses you, and captivates you, pushes you with the force of youth. Life is a bunch of beauties if your love is by your side. The sky seems so close, that a star is in your hand. A star like the one you love.*"

I tell Dante: "If only you knew how I adore you."

He tells me: "You are beautiful like the sun; full of perfume, like a flower."

The words of the tango, *Balada Para un Loco*, come to mind and I tell them to him: "*I know I am crazy, crazy, crazy.*

*Love me the way I am: crazy, crazy, crazy. Climb up into my insane tenderness. Don a wig of larks on your head and fly! Fly with me now! Come! Open up your love, we are going to attempt the crazy magic of reviving. Let's go flying on my super sport illusion. Come, fly, feel the crazy desire I have for you. The nuts who invented love: an angel, a soldier and a girl gave us this dance. Love me the way I am. Only you can see me. Come. Dance. Fly.*"

And he does!

One kiss and my spirits are up—up and away. Kisses have wings. Two tongues meet and it's glorious and hot with meaning. I receive my partner's majestic French kiss as I would receive a king's. I want the Lord of my flesh to lord over me. He knows my weaknesses and celebrates them. I know his weaknesses and celebrate them. How easy it is to please me. I'm a cavewoman, and he's the fire I just discovered. The world will never be the same again. Stars have to keep their distances. (Do not touch.) His heavenly body makes no such demand. (Thank God!) He is the man I ran up the church steps to wed. And would do it a second, a third and a fourth time. My mate is gorgeous and absolutely delicious. I am covetous of his vigour and youthful good looks. It is as if his body had simply dressed up his spirit (had kept it nice & warm) and now that he's totally undressed, I can finally have my way with him. Because his tongue is inside my mouth, I am a life giver, a challenger of spirits: faith, hope and charity.

Mr. Dante Aglieri and Sophie Wolfe are re-united. Thank the Lord.

As darkness sets in, the moon rises, and the man in my arms drives my heart crazy with freedom.

"Can you feel the crazy desire I have for you?" I say.

"Love me, and you *un-love* me," he says.

Another riddle I don't understand. Who wants to solve it? Not me. I'm too hot, too involved, too juiced up to care. I promise him I will respect him in the morning—I swear my life on it.

The deal is this, he says, one fuck and you'll be satisfied—healed, you know.

Oh please, please, please cure me, I tease, but I sense there's a catch and I won't like it.

To seize suffering, he says, you must stop the origin of the suffering.

Yes, but ...

Craving something or someone you can't have does you no good, Dante tells me. To achieve joyfulness or serenity you have to be emancipated from your craving.

Yes, but ...

Love creates harmony, he says. For every action, a reaction. For every love lost, another must be found.

I disagree.

"You must forget me," he says.

"I can't and I won't," I say.

"It's not your choice," he says putting his hands up my skirt, his lips on mine, making dialogue impossible; weakening my resistance, ordering my flesh to respond to his, even though I don't want to. Because if we make love, I will *un-love* him, meaning (if I got it right) I will do what's expected—get on with my life. Pretend my life wasn't smashed to bits when his was.

Amnesia is a blessing, he says. Ask any immigrant. It helps both the ones who leave their country, and those who remain in it.

Toss out the past? Not me. If I were an immigrant, I would opt for double citizenship.

It's not as simple as that, he says. You can't live in two countries at one and the same time. You can't be awake and asleep at one and the same time.

There is no reason why you can't hold onto the past, and still live in the present, I argue. It's not like you have to choose between two evils: Which city should the enemy be allowed to bomb—Paris or Rome?

You can't hold onto the past for dear life and be happy, he says. Sophie, I need you to be happy. That's all there is to it. I made the choice for you.

He presses himself against me. Kisses have wings and I must spread them out. I am his earth angel, his confidant; his household slut. He insists I put my unemployed lust to good use.

I try to make conversation, bring up the subject of how his car was totalled that terrible night and how he is the one who left me (I didn't leave him!) but he puts his lips on mine and shuts me up. I vaguely remember I came here to solve a murder mystery, but at this point in time, I have no interest in playing detective.

His kisses enchant me. He's a spirit doctor, a medicine man, cleaning up my spirit wounds. The ins and outs of day to day existence don't matter. What matters is that I allow him to be my angel of mercy, administer to me—now. (Forget tomorrow!) What matters is that I give myself up to pleasure.

He strips me of my clothes, my defences, my good sense. Like a woman in a sex game, tied up for a good reason (a slave to passion), like a woman under anaesthesia (a slave to pain), like a woman, an immigrant, abandoning her country and her family (a slave to her dreams), like a warrior, ready to sacrifice her dreams (a slave to what's right), I am lost. I am too sick or too full of lust to say no; my mouth, my skin, my thoughts are too full of his spirit to deny him. I put my hands in the air (oh happy victim) and give myself up.

PART IV

# Picture Books

*If a baby laughs in its sleep*
*he laughs with the angels.*

—AN ITALIAN PROVERB

# Chapter 25

When you are shopping for antiques, what you are really after is permanence. Or sacred symbols. Enter an antique shop and you enter a merry world; everything in it will increase in value. If you buy it, it will (you hope) outlive you.

I open the cash register and reopen myself to a new way of life. I can take up pottery or sand art, or anything I like. The important thing is to act; action is superior to thought. "Living in an imaginary world (or in the past) is immoral," says a voice in my head. I don't know to whom the voice belongs. It could be what philosophers call the higher self. Some would even call the higher self one's guardian angel.

It's Monday. The weather is good, I'm in good health, and my clothes are brand new. The old Sophie wore vintage clothing, not this lady.

I attend to the business at hand. A film production crew wants to pick up some props. Almost everything in the store is for rent. Renting period pieces is a big part of our business now. Hollywood can turn Montréal into Manhattan or Berlin in a wink. The Dream Factory gives us fake cities, fake landscapes, fake time travels, but it's all in good fun. Possibly the most important journey comes after one dies, but that's neither here nor there. Confucius noted: "*While you do not know life, what can you know about death?*" And he's right. When the present presents itself, you've got to grab it by the balls. (Reality's coarse, but what of it?)

On the counter: a 19th century vinegar and oil set (two-in-one). Does this world (the third planet from the sun) and the Otherworld lie side by side (as do the oil and vinegar)? The two can't mix, until God, the Master Chef, pours the contents out, and then *voilà*—what a lovely dish! A Caesar salad cannot compare.

You can fish for food. You can fish for compliments. Natives built nets to catch dreams. Let's go fishing. Let's fish for God. God is a treasure chest filled with IOUs. God is either nothing or God is everything. God is either in the Otherworld or God is the Otherworld, which doesn't say much. But then no one knows if God is more like a man with a gun or a baby looking for a milk mother. I smell the scent of God nearby. Flowers can't hide their divinity. Humans do it all the time.

Do I feel nostalgic for the Otherworld because I passed through it? Probably not. Memory is unreliable as a source of information. Memory is like a dream. Or a phobia. It plays tricks—you can't trust it. Actually there is no point in brooding about the past, or fantasizing about the future. (Eternity is a sure thing?) Calling a friend, calling your mother, painting a pretty picture, composing an aria, writing down a recipe, any act is better than hoping and wishing life is not as short as all that. (Is it?) *Carpe diem*.

I think of my late husband and I smile. It's almost a knee-jerk reaction. Have no pain. No sad thoughts. No bad dreams ... Mary, Mary had a little lamb; Sophie, Sophie had a little miracle.

"I'm pregnant," I tell my boss.

"Who is the father?" he asks.

"Dante."

"That can't be," he says.

"I was pregnant long before Dante died, but I didn't know it. I nearly miscarried in my fourth month, haemorrhaging badly, nearly dying, but luckily the baby was unharmed. Everything's fine."

"That's wonderful," he says, and I know he means it.

*Dearest baby,*

*Come live in my world, in my house, in my body. Enjoy me. Have a nice swim. A nice dance. Anything you like. Everything I own is yours for the asking.*

*Affectionately yours, your mom-to-be,*
*Sophie Wolfe*

*My dearest child,*

*A summer day full of colour is worth the long trip. Promise.*

*Love and kisses,*
*Mommy*

*Sweet baby,*

*Come force yourself into the Milky Way and make claims on it. Come defend your right to exist; my wishing you, gives you all sorts of rights, come make good on them.*

*Baby-baby, find me and thrill me or find me and do nothing.*

*Your servant,*
*Sophie Wolfe*

*Dear baby,*

*I promise to bring you into the sunlight; I promise to create you. The sky has to be shared. It's so big and glorious. Come and take a look.*

*Lovingly yours,*
*Sophie Wolfe*

*Miracle child,*

*Come and enjoy the show of your own making. Come create yourself.*

*Forever yours,*
*Mommy*

Life speeds up. Days, weeks, months fly out the window and go down south, migrating to warm temperatures, warm feelings—fertile landscapes. A magic world.

A baby's here in my body; she's more than an idea my brain is concocting. She's here in my body; a beautiful spirit in the making. What a sweetheart of a deal: I lend her my body for a few months and in return I become a fertility goddess. (Which mom isn't?)

I will live through her. My late husband will live through her. The magic continues. My baby is the magician and the rabbit in the hat. My sun, my moon, my artificial light, my ridiculous joy. Stars help us see in the dark; help drivers change lane; help yachtsmen steer clear of rocky shores. I don't know when a new star is born, but then I don't need to know, so many of them, up there, advertising God is Good.

Am big with life, big like an ocean liner—so much life is in me. It's not just one baby physically present, but dozens of generations that are here, hundreds of passengers are waiting in line. I feel nauseous, as if I were actually present on a ship, riding big waves. Everyone starts off on international waters—womb waters are as mighty as the Atlantic; travelling from non-existence to existence is quite a journey.

I shouldn't get melancholic. Dante wouldn't want me to. I shouldn't drink the excellent Italian wine one can find in every corner shop in Montréal and I don't. (I don't want my baby to get drunk, poison her with false images of our world, she deserves better.) This is Dante's baby and I will do whatever I must to protect her. (I know it's a girl, I was shown her picture!) Possibly, there's something to ancestor worship—all of us (the dead & the living) are taking care of each other, promising, the best is yet to come.

The birth of a new star, miraculous *et al*, can't compete with a baby's wish for life. Even a ne'er-do-well's wish to turn his life around can't compare to a baby's wish to come into our world. The creation of a new star starts with a big bang; we can't hear the noise. I hear my baby's wish to come to life. Birth pre-dates conception; when someone is wished for that's the moment the process begins. Too bad a wish can't be photographed. Because that's the baby's first real moment in this world. An ultrasound image is more like an afterthought.

"There's your baby," says my doctor, pointing out her hands, feet. And beating heart on the screen.

On the table: goodwill.

The Aglieris thank me for not asking for Dante's share of the family restaurant, *Chez Nina*. Now that the insurance money has come through, *Chez Nina* will be up and running in no time.

Presently, dinner is served and the quality of the home-cured *prosciutto* discussed, or rather, argued over—Dante's father suggesting it is the best they've made, but his wife is not so sure: "Last year, it was less salty."

"I love *prosciutto*," I tell Michele, and to his mother, I say the same, but in her mother tongue.

"*Bravo. Sei veramente italiana,*" she tells me. No smile, no nothing.

Everyone else, though, reacts with excitement. And just because I spoke a few words of Italian. You'd think I had just broken an Olympic record.

Dante's sister, Lina, is so impressed, she calls in her daughter from the other room and demands I repeat my feat. If an *Inglese* could speak Italian, her daughter could too!

I tell the family I'm pregnant. And that's when I know for sure I won—not one gold medal, but half a dozen at the Aglieris' Olympic games.

"Michele, please convince your parents that, as much as I love their *prosciutto*, I've had enough."

"Everyone, but you, calls me Mike," he says, apparently convinced that by Italianizing his name I think less of him.

Someone turns on the TV and there is Dante's uncle on the six o'clock news. His conviction for tax fraud and other charges has been overturned. He's a free man. His lawyer is considering suing the press for defamation of character. Franco Aglieri should not have to shoulder the blame for the corruption and collusion that is festering in Québec's construction industry. He has always conducted himself with honesty and integrity. And because of it, or in spite of it, his client plans to give a handsome sum to an Italian orphanage run by Mother Theresa's Sisters of Charity.

"The poor do not need pity," Franco Aglieri tells the reporter. "They need love. No one can be too kind or too gentle."

I think to myself: when Mother Theresa was alive she didn't have any qualms about taking money from gangsters to pay for her good works. Everyone and everything can be redeemed. Or transformed. Leaves. Sorrow. Even evil can be made use of.

Violence is built into the universe. (Stars are *de facto* bombs—it's just that the explosions are happening far away from us.) One couldn't wish upon a star if it didn't have muscle power to back it up.

Michele—Mike—butts into my thoughts and assures

me that his uncle (despite what I and everyone else might think) isn't and never was part of the Mafia. "Some of the members of my uncle's family in Sicily may have made their fortune from drug trafficking, illegal gambling and prostitution, but that's not how he got rich. In 2014 despite the rhetoric that we're all equal under the law, despite the government push to make us all clones of each other: speak the same language, dress in the same way, abide by the same cultural traditions and pray to the same God, the fact is that our family name still defines who we are. It brands us. Our skin colour does it as well, but that's visible, those in power don't dare use it against us. (That would be breaking the law!). But there are no laws which make it illegal to discriminate against those with foreign-sounding names. If your name can't be linked to the nation's founding fathers, you're out of luck. You will not get a government job or a government contract, unless of course, you are willing to stuff an envelope with cash and offer it to those in charge."

"Is that what your uncle did? Did he stuff an envelope with cash? Is that how he got the go-ahead to build Montreal's new super-hospital?" I ask.

"If he did, he's not saying. Nor is anyone complaining. Montréal's businessmen are bullied into breaking the law by the very individuals who were elected to uphold it. The Mayors of Montréal and Laval resigned as a direct result of revelations made in the Charbonneau Commission, but will their resignation change anything? The culture of political corruption predates the Mafia. Predates Confederation. Native Americans were offered bribes and gifts—didn't the government of France buy the island of Montréal for a song?"

What's he saying? Franco Aglieri, one of Canada's richest men, has no connections to the underworld? It was all in my head?

Mike tells me: "My grandfather was a bricklayer. Both his sons learned the trade, but my uncle, unlike my father, became a contractor. His business did well. He did nothing illegal. You don't have to take my word for it. Ask your mother. She decided to cancel the show she was going to do on the Montréal Mafia because she couldn't dig up any dirt on my uncle. Besides, I told her I didn't want to work for her. I like being a chef."

I never thought of myself as being prejudiced against Italians, but am I? Prejudice blindfolds you to the truth. Is it possible to take the blindfold off? Become tolerant, impartial and trusting? Or is it impossible to ever see things as they are? Truth is more like a seeing-eye dog, it helps steer you in the right direction. But even when it does, you are still at a disadvantage. No one can see the future. Nor the past. And that interferes with the view. The present is a touch out of focus. You have to always step back, and ask, "What would Jesus (or the Buddha) do? And if you don't want to look to religious leaders for advice, you can always turn to Shakespeare. He did say: "*To err is human; to forgive, divine.*"

I help myself to another slice of *prosciutto* and melon. The two together are better than either one apart. The same can be said when two cultures meet and mate.

# Chapter 26

My daughter delivers me out of the ordinary and into a magic world. Joy no longer surprises me. I wake up and I do what I must, and take pleasure in it.

Newscasters talk of civil wars and uncivil acts, but I don't care to listen. To live is a duty. To live well is a privilege. (Thus speaks my baby's smile.) You can always count on a baby to give you good news.

Mother's office is abuzz with activity. Everyone comes in at the same time, as if a church bell had been rung—time for mass. On the agenda: next week's show—on doubles or *doppelgangers*. The reason I'm here is because I'm going to be a guest on the show. The host made good on her promise—the show's resources were used to track down my double.

Is it possible I have a twin? I fantasized about having a sister, but never a twin. One time, when I was a little girl, my mother took me to an amusement park in Rome, and there, in the House of Mirrors, I saw distorted images of myself. It was unnerving. Could I live in a world where I had dozens of Sophies, staring back at me, reminding me I was not unique?

A senior staff member seems to have read my thoughts as she suggests that the show on doubles could include other related topics, such as clones and cyborgs. Researchers who worked on Dolly, the sheep, the first cloned mammal, could be interviewed. Modern cloning techniques have successfully reproduced pigs, cats, dogs and horses. Anyone with enough cash can now order an exact genetic copy of his beloved pet.

"I like that idea," says my mother. "The ethics of human cloning could be debated on the show. One day humans might be cloned for the sole purpose of providing organ donations. People could live forever. With the advent of artificial intelligence, machines will do all the work, and then what will humans do?"

"Make babies, not war?" I suggest.

Silence.

A Concordia student, an intern, tells the group that according to her research seeing one's double is not an uncommon experience. Theorists suggest the para-psychological phenomenon can be ascribed to hysteric delusion. Otto Rank considered seeing one's double as a symptom of narcissism.

The senior staff member doesn't buy into Otto Rank's theories. The suggestion has been made our bodies have two sets of central nervous systems, one inside our body (which is visible), and one outside it (which is invisible).

The one outside our bodies contains all our memories and thoughts in code. And this is what survives after death. Jesus Christ multiplied loaves and fishes; people, people; flowers, flowers, etc. There's an inner drive to reproduce. Copy. Duplicate ...

The staff of *Sandra Live* continue to dish out ideas assembly-line style, one after the other—the segment on doubles is to include (yes, no, maybe?): identical twins, clones, and/or celebrity look-alikes?

My mother has an opinion. (She always does.) "Everyone wants to be famous. And if they can't be famous, they want to be associated with those who are. And if they can't do that, then they'll wear the same clothes, eat in the same restaurants, and do whatever they can to copy those who are famous. Copying people is a growth industry. The irony is that this is happening at the same time the cult of the individual is at its highest."

A Marilyn Monroe female impersonator is brought in and interviewed.

"I don't believe you're a man," my mother says, challenging the sex kitten. The impersonator takes her hand and puts it on his vital area.

Can we do this on camera? someone asks. Laughter.

And then my double on screen—via satellite. The double's materialization usually means the soul has escaped the body and death is imminent. To be continued ... Transmission problems.

Live from *la Ville de Montréal* ... Canada's Queen of Small Talk.

*Sandra Live* lives up to its reputation—anything goes. The host will even bring in her own daughter and prove she's open and caring, and a single mom (for real!).

Prompters prompt: applause!

On screen: Sophie Wolfe's double in living colour.

Off screen: my doubts. Recorded images can be altered and distorted.

On screen. Prompters prompt: applause.

Here she comes—my double, in person!

The shock of the week. Or of the decade (for me)!

My double, a school teacher from Bethlehem, Massachusetts, looks like me (well, almost), sounds like me (not exactly, but close enough), but is she my twin? Yes, no ... The envelope please. DNA testing has proved without a shadow of a doubt that ... Commercial break.

Off screen: Doubting Thomas relays her suspicions. Was Papa Bear a big hairy ape? Why can't he be found?

"You hate me," says big Mamma Bear.

"I admire you, mother."

"It's the nicest thing you ever said to me," she says, real tears in her eyes.

"I can't know who I am, unless I know who my father is," I tell her.

"I know who my father is and I don't have a clue to who I am," she says. "When I changed my name from Tremblay to Wolfe, my father nearly disowned me. Here I was in Italy, working for Radio-Canada, a card-carrying PQ member, fighting for Québec to become an independent country, and my father could not forgive me because I had changed my name. Did I want to re-brand myself as an Anglophone? He traced his ancestry back to Champlain.

Then he died, and the question of my ethnicity stopped haunting me. I refused to think of myself as half-French and half-English, living in an in-between world called, Solitude. I am what I am and that's good enough."

"It's not your father I asked you about, but mine," I remind her.

"How many times do I have to tell you the story? My doctor had told me I would never have a baby because I had the same predisposition to miscarry as did my mother. The month you were conceived I was on the road, travelling from Milan to Palermo. I went to bars and enjoyed the attention of men whose names I did not care to know. My mother had died that year and I couldn't bear to be alone at night. You can imagine the rest."

"Were the men Italian?"

"For the most part."

"You could have had an abortion."

"My mother had 8 miscarriages. She would have given anything for another child. She couldn't have one, and so I did. It was my gift."

"But she was dead!"

"Those you love don't die. My mother is as real to me today as when I was a little girl and she walked me to school. There I was ten years old, all the other kids managed to get to school on their own, but my mother insisted I hold her hand until we got to the door of the building."

"Your staff went through a lot of trouble and expense to find my double."

"And why do you think I did it? To up my ratings? Sophie, I need you to love me."

Prompters prompt....

On screen: Sandra Wolfe turns to the camera and with a stone face reveals the results of the DNA testing. They prove without a shadow of a doubt that Miss Bethlehem, Massachusetts and her daughter, Sophie Wolfe, are not related by blood. She could be anybody.

On screen: My double smiles. And so do I.

My daughter thinks I'm her guardian angel but I know better. My daughter is helping me understand that, as much as we want our mothers to be above reproach (to be better than us—kinder, gentler etc.), they're not. (Just look at me!) Only when we become mothers ourselves can we forgive our mothers for being imperfect. It hits me—here I was all these years resenting my mother for failing to provide me with a father, a sister, a traditional nuclear family setup, and now it turns out my own daughter won't have any of these things either. Should I have said no to motherhood?

Finally I understand there are two sides to every story. Okay, I knew it before, but now my gut knows it. Only when that happens can you free yourself and do the honourable thing—be kind. It's the law of God. And if it isn't, it's definitely the law as prescribed by Confucius, Moses, Jesus and the Buddha. Unconditional love requires a superhuman effort, but it doesn't take all that much to be kind.

Ice cream is easy to love. Babies are too. Later on, you need a miracle to soften you up. You can't always make yourself sweet to the taste, but, I guess, you win points for trying.

At *Chez Nina*, sitting outside, on the newly-renovated

terrace, my mother offers my daughter her first taste of ice cream. She's in heaven. And so am I (because she is!).

I eat and mother talks (The usual). My mother says something about celebrities wearing their fame like religious habits. There's a stench of holiness about them. You can't look at them and not wonder what it's like to live in a world where your every word counts. That's my mother for you—she'll never admit she herself belongs to the new religious order. Pop icons, Madonna look-alikes, female impersonators, ventriloquists, etc., have graced her show (church?), but she'll always take the backseat. Possibly that's why her show is so popular—she identifies with the little guy, on his knees, ready to venerate the strange and beautiful. This might be the very reason I have never accepted her—she's too much like me—she's vulnerable. (Her fame camouflages it, of course, but behind the designer clothes, she is just a little girl, eager to please.) When she's on camera she's bubbly; off-camera she's reclusive, shy almost. Put a camera in front of her and she opens up as if the camera were a life support system. She is the first to admit it too; like an invalid, she can't live without being hooked up to an iron lung: her audience ... And to think I thought a mother had to be in a class of her own, above suspicion, holy like. Silly old me.

A mother is anyone and everyone, the point being that the beginning and end of life don't come nicely wrapped up, meaning, mothers are gods and ungodly, and sometimes god-awful—living contradictions, like everyone else. And, if the truth hurts, mothers will be the first ones to lie through their teeth. If that's good or bad, you tell me.

# Chapter 27

The phone rings and it's for Mrs. Aglieri.

It's the police. The driver who rammed into my husband's car has been identified, I'm told. Another murder mystery solved.

The culprit was a victim himself. A victim of Alzheimer's. The 90-year-old recently passed away, but witnesses have come forward and placed him at the scene of the crime.

Another hit-and-run solved. Another police file closed. Another widow mystified.

During *la Settimana Italiana di Montreal* most shops and buildings in the municipality display Italy's tricolored flag; in *la citta di San Leonardo*, the "real" *Piccola Italia*, the national symbol is in evidence all-year round. At Complexe Aglieri, where my daughter and I take the elevator to the 4th floor, *il Tricolore* dominates the décor. Some believe that

Italian cuisine inspired the use of the flag's three colours, but personally I prefer the religious interpretation: green represents hope, white represents, faith and red represents, charity. Olives, tomatoes and garlic may be divine in origin, but now that Italians, like the rest of the known world have developed a palette for international dishes, they are *not* what they eat.

My daughter's first visit to the dentist is uneventful, except the staff do make a fuss over her, as does Guido, until the secretary tells him his mother is on the phone and could he speak to her? He leaves the room, and when he returns, he has such a sad look on his face, I imagine the worse.

"My mother couldn't stop crying," he tells me. "My sister's children stayed overnight at her place, and this morning, she couldn't understand what it is they wanted for breakfast. My nephews only speak French, and my mother only speaks English. Here she was in the same position as her own unilingual Italian mother, my nonna, had been when she married and had children. Except my nonna had it a bit easier as she had grown up in the old country and had incorporated its values. Her mother, my nonna knew who she was, but what was she, she wanted to know? She was neither English nor Italian, and she certainly wasn't French. She was living between 2 worlds, she said. No one could see her or hear her."

"Do any Montrealers feel at home?" I ask. "My grandmother was English, and my grandfather, French. I don't belong in either group. I thought if I could create myself in my own image, I would be free. But it's not possible. Like that tango (*Amarras*) says: *'Today I'm nothing. I only know that*

*I suffered. I look for courage to leave, to get away, but I live tied to my past. Memories chain me. I'm like a coal boat that has been on the bank. It doesn't sail anymore.*'"

"You don't need a boat," Guido says. "Your daughter will give you wings."

"She is my angel of love."

"There is a careless beauty about her," Guido notes and I agree.

He plays with her fingers, and she develops a curious attachment to his big fat chewy ones.

My daughter puts Guido's ring finger in my mouth.

"Bite it," he tells me, "if you think you can ... love me ... just a little."

My teeth dig into his flesh; why, I am not sure.

I tell Guido: "The first time you fall in love, you take it for granted; you're at home, in your own country. Falling in love the second time has an element of risk. It's a bit like being an immigrant—choosing the New World over the Old one. Part of you remains behind too, attached to the Old World; its rural settings. Still, the New World has more to offer than the old one; that's why you chose it."

"I don't expect you to choose me, Sophie. I smell of the Old World. It has the stink of defeat."

Suddenly I want his lips to close in on mine and empower me. Turn me into a warrior. Or, better yet, a healer. This man needs his wounds tended to, and I could do it. I could be of use.

When you're opening a gift, turning on the light, travelling abroad or falling in love, you don't take anything for granted. When Guido's divorce comes through, the surprise is part of the pleasure.

While my daughter is asleep in a beautiful world of her own making, I make my old flame breakfast. What shall it be: English muffins or French toast? Eggs Benedict or angel cake? There's a recipe for everything. Whip up a bit of star-dust in a bowl and there's your universe. Only God knows the right proportions; still, it's all in the recipe. There you have it—cooking is the oldest interactive game of all time.

How old is the universe? How old is God? Is God older than the universe? If the Big Bang hadn't happened 15 billion years ago, I wouldn't be here. So does that make me as old as time?

Transformations take place in the kitchen; a little flour and sugar, a couple of eggs, and you have a cake to die for. Can our bodies be transformed: go from a two-cell entity to a multi-celled thinking creature, from child to back-stabbing teen, from middle-aged woman to sage to spirit?

I ask Guido: "Is there life after death?"

"Why shouldn't there be?" he replies. "This is the first time in history people don't believe in Heaven. I can understand why one wouldn't want any gods around. Hierarchical systems are anti-democratic, but not to believe in Heaven lacks imagination. Flowers don't have imagination. Cats and dogs don't have imagination. Nor do animals in the wild. Eat or be eaten, and that's it. But to think that a thinking creature could be satisfied with a few years of good health. How pitiful!"

He plants a kiss on the nape of my neck and says: "If you're real lucky you travel first class with a man you adore by your side, but if you're unlucky like you were, you have to do it second class. That doesn't mean you don't get to visit London or Paris; you just do it on a budget. The important thing is that you get there."

"It's possible to love two countries, two cities, two men—one is just as good as the other. I cared for Dante. And I care for you—equally."

"Thank you."

"Why do you love me?" I ask. "And don't say it's because you like to fuck me, because it won't count."

"You're a bit like the tango—captivating, rebellious and overly sweet."

"And?"

"You intrigue me. Some days you behave like you're 12 and others, 112. I never know whom I'll be with—a young girl or a wise fool."

"Is life a comedy, or a tragedy?" asks the wise fool.

"Is life more like an episode of 'The Sopranos' or 'I Love Lucy'? It all depends whether the leading man gets to play the part of Ricky Ricardo, a musician, or Tony Soprano, a hit man. You decide."

"You didn't answer the question. And don't tell me life is more like an episode of 'The Twilight Zone' than a comedy or a tragedy because I don't like fantasy."

"You know as well as I do life is comic and tragic at the same time."

"A typical Italian answer. It's never a yes or a no. Always yes and no. Or a maybe."

"There's no science to living, or loving. The science of love is more like a branch of metaphysics, which is to say, it's more like a pseudo-science, in which case, there are no rules—anything goes."

"Meaning?"

"You don't have to be the first to cross the Atlantic in

a small boat or be first at anything to win someone's affection. You can be ordinary and be loved. If it can happen to me, it can happen to anyone."

"Enough talk," I say. "Help me cook."

Well, oh, um ... umm ... it's his day off, and well, umm ... he doesn't like to cook, and besides, he has other things on his mind ...

Like?

A ghetto is still a ghetto, even if there are lots of big houses in it. It's time Italians expand their borders and move in with the natives. Most of his clients come to him because he's Italian, but his nationality shouldn't be at issue. If he's good, he's good, period. That's why he would like to open an office downtown.

Arguments that he has lived and worked in an Italian neighbourhood all his life don't sit well with him.

I tell him: "Odd—you want to be Canadian, and I want to be Italian. Everyone assumes immigrants are assimilated into the dominant culture, but often, the reverse happens. No more melting pots. Lots of side dishes."

Tasting the batter, he says: "You can't cook and you want to be Italian when you grow up?"

I turn on the radio. A golden oldie blasts out: "Devil or angel dear, whichever you are, I love you."

No one is too old or too young or too educated or too poor to be awed. Call awe an automatic response. Or a primitive response to the Divine. No technology is advanced enough to take a picture of God. You have to use your imagination. Or, better yet, go to a firework display and see the Light.

Fireworks are a communal feast for the eyes, all of us gazing, eating up the celestial ice cream, no complaints. Easy to digest. (Those with lactose intolerance need not worry.)

Watching the sky spectacle, waiting for the next splash of colour, we cannot but approve of each other; in the dark imperfections are glossed over. A woman in a wheelchair will forget about her disability; she and the universe are alike—both are works-in-progress. A woman without a head on her shoulders will go out and rent one for the evening just so she can celebrate the invention of gunpowder. Boom, boom, boom ...

The night sky is a warrior, defending her message: peace and joy. When the celestial show of force occurs, elements break down, explode—and so what was, now isn't ...

Light shows aren't particularly sexy, unless, of course, your partner is watching it with you (mine is), in which case the fireworks represent the birth of a new star; in which case, you're talking about additions rather than subtractions and that's sexy enough. During a celestial show of force, nature adds things together; during sex couples also add things together (e.g., I love yous).

During sex each partner puts his or her hunger to good use. "Come on, Honey, taste me," one might tell the other, and then the carnal fireworks start. Boom, boom, boom. Celestial light shows have mass audiences. Lovemaking has no need for spectators. Like prayer, it suspends judgement. You can't sin when you're giving yourself up to the man you love whom you need as much as you need your lungs.

God is forever busy making love with the universe; busy, busy, busy procreating little ones, but what of it? God is far away and my partner is close by, forever willing to give me pleasure—any which way I please. (Lucky for me he now likes oral sex as much as I do.) You don't need fireworks to be amazed; plenty of oohs and aahs readily available in the bedroom with the moon and the stars peeking through the window.

When you are busy kissing, you are too busy feeling nice and comfortable in your beautiful little body to worry about nasty diseases, enemies; self-hate. When you are being kissed as I am presently being kissed you are full of possibilities—an upcoming pop star or The Mother of the Year. You are full of untapped talents; they're hiding in your body, ready to blossom each time you are kissed. When you are kissed you are given hope that you are more than meets the eye. Each time you are kissed the flowering of self-love takes place. It allows you to tap dance on your vulnerabilities and become your own lord and master.

Age is no barrier to kissing, to coming together and declaring that you are devoted admirers of each other. When you are being kissed, attended to, cared for, your little comfort zone gets bigger and bigger—from the size of a room to the size of a continent. Soon enough you will find yourself believing Heaven is a geographical location where you will meet your relatives and tell them how glad you were that they were part of your life, as well as a place where you will continue to make love and be attended to with kisses from head to toe, and licked to orgasm ...

In every "I love you," a prayer; in every endearment, grace, and in every thank you, genesis, the promise of life after life.

"Say after me," I tell my partner. "I love you moon, I love you, Mr. Big Dipper. Be mine tonight and I'll be yours."

And he does.

# Chapter 28

On my wedding day the earth is a cathedral, the sky, its dome; *la Ville de Montréal* is an oversized tabernacle, its old buildings, chalices, *le Vieux-Port*, holy water. Within its doors, men and women are whiling away the time, playing cards, playing basketball, watching old movies, getting fat; praying sometimes. On my wedding day I can't imagine a future without an unlimited supply of good times.

Walking down the aisle, pampered and absolved of all sin, bad memories, bad experiences, with every cell of my body alert and ready for action—everything is as it should be. There is mom and her entourage of best friends, smiling, and to her left, there is Guido's super big family; missing are my friends (don't have any!) but no matter. On my wedding day I am sure I will make some friends real fast and then I will invite them over for cake and coffee and be like everyone else—gloriously happy. Actually, right this moment I am gloriously happy. I can't imagine anything better than this ...

Vows taken, rings exchanged, standing outside the *Basilique Notre-Dame*, I am a success story-in-the-making, another Celine Dion super rock star look-alike who managed to convince the Vatican that the groom's first marriage had to be annulled, and am now ready to take on the world by storm—the standard thing. On my wedding day (stupid me!) nothing is the standard thing. I can hear the words, "I love you," over and over again and love them more each time. They're part of my treasured bridal trousseau.

On my wedding day business thrives in *le Vieux Montréal*; everywhere I turn I see smiling vendors and their assistants being served by their clients—yes, yes, on my wedding day role reversals are the norm. The unexpected is to be expected. Love demands it. Love is a tyrant—if it sees a frown on someone's face, it has to go; love gives out smiles and wearers have to put them on. (You can't see a couple in love and not smile!) For the first time in my life I can appreciate why the words "like" and "love" aren't synonyms; when you like someone, it changes you, but when you love someone it changes you and everyone around you as well. Love changes the viewer and the viewed; everything is transformed and enveloped in the supernatural—God is in your eyes and because of it *la vita è bella.*

I step into a horse-drawn carriage and smile for the camera. The driver gives no hint of being tired or undervalued; he does not have that look of distaste, common among the working class. I swear even the old horses pulling his carriage are smiling, glad to be of use, using their muscle power to entertain human-un-kind. Few know it but horses can laugh, can talk, can pray; the problem is unless you are crazy and in love you wouldn't be able to understand Horse language. (It's far too complex for humans' little brains.)

On my wedding day everything on this rocky planet called Earth is in working order. The earth is no longer a big place, but a cathedral, tangible and easy to clean; everything is sacred. Everyone's radiating good health, good feelings. Am I manic? Better believe it. You can't see auras unless you're in a dream state or madly in love. Even when you don't have a religion to call your own (I don't), love transforms the planet. It's no longer a big place, but a beautiful cathedral where you can't be alone because God is with you.

Well, it looks like my falling for my old flame was a real fall (literally)—it made me delirious; possibly when I recover from the fall I will have to re-acknowledge things are what they are (servants are not served by their masters!). But never you mind. On my wedding day humdrum existences are lifted and seen for what they are: blessed. Love encompasses the solar system, the Milky Way and its one billion stars. (Divine inspiration at its best!)

Actually, on my wedding day, I can't call the earth a *cathedral* and be satisfied—the word, *cathedral*, is too restrictive. I must go back and correct my thinking. I should call the earth *a place of worship.* The earth could be a temple or a synagogue or a Native longhouse or any other sacred place. That said, the word, *sacred*, is also too restrictive. *Sacred* is too serious a word. A wedding is both serious and not serious. It's a time for merriment. Brides and grooms deserve a world where there is no pain. On my wedding day I should compare the earth to a *house* rather than to a place of worship. Let me call the earth *mia casa, our house.* The former isn't a direct translation of the latter, but who cares? On my wedding day there are no words to describe the earth, nor are there adequate words for love. The more you love the less certain words become. In the beginning was the word, and in the end, a joyful exclamation point!!!!!!!!!!!!!!!!!

First feat: the bride, *The Champion of Left Feet*, gets to the dance floor without bumping into anyone.

Second feat: *The Champion of Left Feet*, Sophie Wolfe, gets through the first dance without stepping on her groom's toes.

Someone says: "You dance well. Did you take lessons?"

Everyday miracles are hard to document.

All I know is that this bride couldn't tell her left foot from her right and now she can tango like a pro.

The Vatican might not think of it as a feat (let alone a miracle) but this bride sure does!

Rather stare into my beloved's eyes than into a mirror. His eyes don't see me as I am—my nose is shortened, my lips enhanced, my skin—my smile—smoothed out. Come-as-you-like. Love is the best plastic surgeon on this side of the Atlantic. Love doesn't charge a penny or use invasive surgery. When I see the world through his eyes, it's cleaner, holier—more like him.

# Chapter 29

Winter carnivals can cheer you up, but stay away from *le Carnaval di Quebéc* and Montréal's *Igloofest*. Our below-freezing temperatures will ruin your appetite for good sex.

Go to Brazil if you can afford it and, if you can't, stay put and use your imagination and who knows where you'll land.

Come to Montréal in the summertime. In the summer our sky gleams as if an army of cleaning women had just washed it. You can see your reflection in it if you look hard enough. Just don't make the mistake and think you see angels in the vicinity because then they'll put you in the loony bin. But don't you worry; come to Montréal in the summertime and angels will be the last thing on your mind. Clowns, jugglers, fire-eaters and jazz musicians will compete for your attention. At every turn a gay parade. Come to Montréal in the summertime and experience a carnival atmosphere, *sans* the cold. Watch out though for the animals behind the circus tents, reading books or guzzling beer.

If they have their way, they'll blow their own horn. And what next?

Venetians have to make do with Vivaldi & Co.; Parisians have one composer and if you don't know who he is stay out of town; New Yorkers are too busy playing the stock market to care about music.

Montréal is the jazz capital of the world and for good reason. There are so many languages spoken on the island something had to be done. Montréal is a veritable Tower of Babel: *Ici on parle*: *Italiano, Espanol, Magyar, Svenska, Filipino,* Chinese and Japanese; Africa has 1,000 languages and you can find most of them spoken here too. Jesus multiplied loaves of bread in Palestine; in Montréal Jesus must be blessing languages. There are more languages spoken per square foot here than any other place in the world. Despite government legislation trumpeting *le français* as the official language, unofficial languages dominate. To facilitate communication between government employees and landed immigrants and migrant workers and refugees and illegal aliens and American imperialists and $4^{th}$ generation British riff-raff, the language on the streets of Montréal is Jazz. The English language has 26 letters, and Jazz has no letters at all, making it easily accessible. All you need is a heart. And if you have a pair of shoes, all you have to do is click your heels, and feel at home. Saint Coltrane has more devotees in Montréal than Saint Brother André. Trumpets and pianos speak up any chance they can. Speak Jazz and break the language barrier.

Some would have you believe Money is the international language, and yes, it is easily mastered and can be picked up anywhere, but if it is a little sophistication you're after,

Jazz is it. Its rhythm is the beat that lives in this city. It does not have pretension. It does not want to be indecent. Its name is Jazz and nothing else. Experience the language of merriment and you can celebrate Christmas in July—peace and joy for one and all. Have a merry Jazz-y Day.

When *le Festival international de Jazz de Montréal* is in town, it can only lead to one thing—sex, and more sex. Jazz-y sex is an all-night affair, boisterous, self-indulgent, and selfishly selfish. Forget the union of two souls, forget the heavenly Heaven of Catholic archbishops and pale-faced Buddhist nuns, jazz-y sex seeks out pleasure for pleasure's sake. In this little corner of Heaven-on-Earth, lovers use their bodies to get closer to God, any which God—Christian, Hindu, Native American, any which one will do. Thank you, Bacchus. Thank you, Jesus. Thank you.

Shut up and kiss me ... Who's talking now?

Helping herself to a beefy Italian tomato from my garden, my next-door neighbour tells me she is doing a consumer survey for a marketing company on angels and advertising. Am I willing to participate in the study?

Sure, I say.

Are the following quotes correctly attributed to the individuals given on the list—True or False?

1) Thomas Aquinas: *God has provided for us by appointing his angels to be our teachers and guides.*
2) John Calvin: *The angels regard our safety, undertake our defence, direct our ways, and*

*exercise a constant solicitude that no evil befalls us.*

3) Pope Pius XII: *Angels are heavenly, pure, and splendid, and yet have been given us to keep us company on our way. Everyone, no matter how humble he may be, has angels to watch over him.*
4) William Blake: *Angels are not angels because they are holier than men, but because they do not expect holiness from one another, but from God alone.*
5) St. Francis de Sales: *Make yourself familiar with angels, and behold them frequently in spirit; for without being seen, they are present with you.*
6) Saint Ambrose: *If these beings guard you, they do so because they have been summoned by your prayers.*
7) Swedenborg: *Angels live in houses … like the dwellings on earth which we call homes, except they are more beautiful. They have rooms, suites and bedrooms all in abundance. They have courtyards and are surrounded by gardens, flower beds and lawns. The environment in which the angels live reflects their inner state and level of spiritual development.*
8) Thomas Aquinas: *Angels are pure intellect, neither male nor female but able to assume whatever form they like.*

My neighbour looks at my answers and grimaces. (Or was that a smile?)

I tell her: "Companies shouldn't use images of angels to sell their stuff. It's indecent. Companies who deny raises to their workers and make mothers suffer have no right to push their wares. The madness must stop. We must be strong to resist what is bad."

She tells me: "Life is like a cup of coffee. On its own it's bitter, but add sugar, and it's to die for."

I look up at the sky, and there I see, or I think I see, a cloud in the shape of a door. An open door. Or is it a sorcerer's clock?

Summer is no time to be a visionary in Montréal. It is better to stay grounded and tend to the garden. The mild weather and soft sunshine make this city the place to be. There's no reason to travel elsewhere. One doesn't have to go to the Otherworld to seek wisdom. Philosopher kings come in many shapes and forms. Mother Nature is one of them. It is not enough to admire her, one has to mimic her. (If one could learn to weave like a spider, the material made would be stronger than steel—it would be able to stop a plane in mid-flight!) Mother Nature provides wisdom and know-how, but can she provide proof there is life after death? And the answer is a definite yes. If one looks through a microscope, one can see things through it one wouldn't have dreamt were there. Little critters come to life under its glass. It makes the idea of resurrection seem strangely plausible.

The moon hangs in the sky like a) a giant apple, b) a soccer ball or c) a Christmas ornament? I can't make up my mind which it is—ball, apple or ornament? The moon looks good enough to eat or play with, and Christmas never looks far off when the full moon is in the sky, decorating it.

How does the moon stay in position? It's hard enough for socks to stay up, how does this heavenly body do it?

None of us could have affixed it to the sky and have it glow-in-the dark too. Don't have the technology for it.

The Soccer Player who threw it up in the air must have been some fierce sports Champion. Or top-notch Gardener.

Apples take over a year to mature, but you can have a moon harvest every day of the year. And best of all anyone who wants to eat of the fruit can (be you the king of rock or a run-of-the-mill drag queen). Unlike the sun (warms some places better than others), the moon makes no distinctions. Or judgements. Everyone on the planet gets the same share of its beautiful light. A delightful light treat. Take a small bite and be content.

I look out my window and sometimes wonder how far is the Otherworld and does it have a moon as thoughtful and as pretty as ours? A kiss puts a quick end to such thoughts. One kiss and you unravel the mysteries of the universe, and if you don't, try another kiss. (That might do the trick!)

# About The Author

Mary Melfi was born in a small town south of Rome. She immigrated with her family to Canada in 1957; in Montréal she attended the local schools. She married, had two children and graduated with a Masters from McGill University. Mary Melfi has published over a dozen books of critically-acclaimed poetry, prose and drama. Her first novel, *Infertility Rites* (Guernica Editions, 1991), was translated into French and Italian. She is best known for her memoir, *Italy Revisited: Conversations with my Mother* (Guernica Editions, 2009). The book offers an intimate look at the social, cultural, religious and work activities of those living in the Italian countryside prior to World War II. Molise's culinary traditions are also investigated, and lovingly celebrated. *Italy Revisited* was translated into Italian (Iannone Editions, 2012). A French translation is in the works. Archival photos and regional Italian recipes can be found on Mary Melfi's website: www.italyrevisited.org. In 2010 Mary Melfi received the "*Giornata Internazionale Della Donna* Award."

RECYCLED
Paper made from recycled material
FSC® C100212
www.fsc.org

Printed in June 2015
by Gauvin Press,
Gatineau, Québec